11-00

‖‖‖‖‖‖‖‖‖‖‖‖‖‖‖‖‖‖
D0966530

KINDERGARTEN DAD

KINDERGARTEN DAD

•

Helen Wingo

AVALON BOOKS
NEW YORK

To Nikki
and her loving parents

Chapter One

Hallie quelled the butterflies beneath her ribcage as the classroom door opened again.

Her teacher's aide looked up. "Another anxious parent," Anna said, with a note of compassion.

"Um," Hallie murmured. She could use a little of Anna's compassion, too. Getting through her first day as a substitute teacher was about like surviving a 6.7 earthquake.

The tall, dark-haired man in the doorway didn't carry a whip and chair, and he was wearing faded jeans and worn boots. But he gripped the hand of a blond-haired youngster and peered at the semicircle of kindergartners with the wariness of a trainer entering a cage of tigers.

The scent of pine followed him before the door closed, shutting out the midday glare of the Southern California sun. He blinked, adjusting his eyes to the change. With his broad shoulders and lean hips, he

1

looked the epitome of masculinity, but his eyes reminded Hallie of a lioness protecting her cub.

Hallie took a breath as if the air high above San Bernardino could calm her anxiety.

She'd accepted the substitute teaching position in the mountain community as a last resort—screenwriters, too, needed food and shelter—and she planned to return to Los Angeles as soon as she had saved enough money to live on. Not that she was wild about smoggy air, clogged freeways, or even the social events she attended in order to "network." But living near the action was necessary, her agent said, if she wanted to sell a screenplay.

Which she did! The goal she'd set as an insecure teenager—a girl who'd worn a made-over dress and thrift shop shoes to the high school prom—hadn't wavered over time.

After her mother's death, she'd grown up watching Cinderella stories on her aunt's small television screen. She couldn't remember what day she'd decided she could write a Cinderella story like the ones on TV, but she did remember optimistically writing her first story on lined notebook paper. Her fingers told the story to a computer now, and she printed the words on a printer, but the story line was the same. A screenplay class in college had helped her put her stories in the proper format, but it had taken four years to get one script optioned. That money was minimal and long gone. So when her day job ended—downsized was the buzz word—she needed work. Yet, each time the classroom door opened, the thought arose that starving in a garret might be have been a better choice.

Hallie smoothed a honey-colored strand in her swept-back hair and stilled an urge to smooth her blouse inside the band of her slacks.

For crying out loud, the man was just another parent. Not only that, he was late. She crossed the room and extended a hand to the wary father. "Mr. Snow. I'm Hallie Ember. Welcome to Pines Day School."

Joshua Snow peered at her with grave, blue eyes and for a moment she wondered if she'd gotten his name wrong. Mrs. Grant had given her a list of parents, and only two hadn't appeared yet. The other one was a mother.

The hand that met hers was large and the grip firm; the feeling made her breath stand at attention. She withdrew her fingers, relaxing imperceptibly when he turned to look at the boy. "This is Nathan," he said.

Hallie knew the boy's name, just as she knew the father's problem. The child suffered from asthma, and his father was extremely reluctant to let Nathan attend school.

"Being a single father might increase his anxiety over his son's health," Mrs. Grant had said. "He's hesitant to let him out of his sight. He's only here because a counselor suggested that socialization with other children might be more beneficial to his son than private tutoring." She'd added, "I hope he likes our school. We need all the students we can get."

From the look in the man's eyes, the principal's assessment had been an understatement, Hallie thought. She risked a glance at the solemn face. An anxiety-laden parent was more than she had bargained for today.

The tremors in her stomach didn't stop her from turning to her prospective student with a whale-sized smile.

Blond hair fell across the small forehead, almost touching the pale lashes wavering over his apprehensive eyes. A red and white striped T-shirt, tucked into the waistband of new jeans, covered his thin chest. The backpack clinging to his shoulders resembled half the new ones she'd seen on her students this morning.

She leaned down. "Welcome to our classroom, Nathan." She extended her hand again, still feeling the odd rush evoked by the touch of the father's hand. She clasped the small fingers of the timid child gently for a brief moment. Then she straightened, keeping her attention focused on the youthful brown eyes. "Do your friends call you Nathan or Nate?"

"Nate," the boy murmured. His voice was so soft Hallie had to lip-read the answer.

"May I call you Nate since I'd like to be your friend?"

The boy nodded and looked at his father. Hallie didn't let her gaze follow the youngster's. She concentrated on the new student.

"Let me show you where to put your backpack."

She led Nate to a row of low shelves, noting that the father had smiled confidently at the boy and remained standing near the doorway. Pulling out a box, she pointed to the name printed on the end. "We were expecting you." Her words earned her a shy grin.

Helping Nate slip the straps of the pack from his arms, she held the plastic crate while he placed it inside.

"This is where you'll put your things when you come to class. The other children are finger-painting. Would you like to join them?"

At his nod, she took him to meet Anna, and waited for him to sit and accept paint supplies. He showed no more anxiety than the average new student, nor was the father's encouraging smile unusual. But she knew it must take courage to enter unfamiliar territory where contact with untested substances could bring on a life-threatening response.

She glanced toward Nate's father. He looked to be three or four years older than Hallie—thirty-one, thirty-two, maybe. His masculine good looks were marred at the moment by the anxiety in his midnight-blue eyes. She wondered how long he'd been a widower. It didn't cross her mind to think of him as divorced. What mother would leave an ailing child, even if she no longer cared for the child's father? Forcefully, she controlled her musing. Too much concern and compassion for one student, or his father, was not in her best interests. She had enough on her plate just getting through this day with some semblance of professionalism. She walked back to join the wary father.

"Mr. Snow—perhaps you'd like to stay and see the children's activities in the classroom and on the playground?" Hallie didn't make her voice too encouraging.

"If I won't be in the way. . . . " He left the sentence open.

"Of course not." She covered her qualms with a congenial tone. Having him stay would add fuel to her already fevered nerves, but making him feel comfortable leaving Nate in her classroom was more important. "There are some adult chairs on the south wall." She indicated them with her hand.

He didn't move away, and Hallie's gaze roamed the classroom restlessly. Conversation wasn't usually difficult for her. Talking to make-believe people in her lonely childhood may have helped. But words she'd carefully cultivated to flow easily at parties and at writers' meetings evaded her. Her gaze paused on the finger-painters. "Nate seems to like the paint session, doesn't he, Mr. Snow?"

Josh nodded, his glance moving away from Nate reluctantly. He smiled at Hallie, as if remembering a social grace. "I think what he really enjoys is being with other children."

In the background, Hallie heard the squeal of a youthful voice and forced herself to remain calm despite the image of paint-spattered opponents dueling atop the coloring table. Anna was with the children. She returned the new kindergarten father's smile graciously. "Aren't there children where you live?"

"On weekends, holidays, and summer vacations."

Hallie raised a quizzical eyebrow politely.

"We live in a campground area in the mountains."

Hallie restrained a gasp of compassion at the idea of him setting up a tent beneath a pine tree. She reined in her thoughts. These days campers lived in double-wide trailers or luxurious motor homes.

"Then you must look forward to the days when Nate has someone to play with," she said cheerfully.

"Not really. Children bring colds and carloads of stuff that might trigger an asthma attack."

Guilt stabbed Hallie. Joshua Snow wasn't into casual humor where his son's health was concerned. A renewed rush of compassion touched Hallie, but she controlled her voice before she spoke. "It must be difficult for you to be constantly on the alert."

The concerned father glanced at his son before he turned his gaze to Hallie. "I don't want you to feel Nate is a time bomb waiting to explode into an asthma attack. Nor do I expect you to be responsible for his health care. Just call me if he starts to wheeze. I plan to stay nearby, and I carry a beeper. I've given the number to the school secretary."

"Of course, Mr. Snow." A breeze of relief fanned Hallie's lungs. Maybe appeasing the anxiety of Nate's father's wouldn't be as difficult as she'd feared.

"Josh. If you're in a hurry to reach me, Josh is shorter." He smiled as if embarrassed at his briskness. "And friendlier."

"Josh." She nodded. The door opened again, and Hallie smiled carefully, excused herself, and moved away. Her eyes were clear and alert when she greeted the last arrival.

* * *

Josh moved farther into the room, his gaze returning to his son's slight figure. He'd followed Nate's spry progress across the classroom. No evidence of the slow, trudging gait of weariness tainted his steps. There was no labored breathing, nor the slightest trace of a wheeze. Now the boy smeared purple paint lavishly over the surface of a sheet of sky-blue construction paper with bright-eyed attention.

Enrolling Nate in school instead of seeking home teachers was the right decision—maybe. He wanted Nate to lead a normal life, as much as possible.

The private school was probably better for Nate. The public school was minimally closer to their home and farther away from a hospital emergency room. The choice of school was for his sake more than Nate's. Until he knew how Nate would react to a new environment, he needed the security of a nearby medical facility.

His gaze drifted to Nate's attractive teacher, watching her greet the newcomers. A young woman in faded shorts and an oversized T-shirt stood inside the doorway, holding a toddler in her arms and trying to keep a three-year-old from following in his brother's footsteps. Hallie Ember turned her charming smile on the frazzled mother, the rebellious preschooler, and the hesitant new student without a sign of stress.

Josh marveled at her patience. She seemed to have a natural instinct for calming nervous youngsters and their anxious parents. To his surprise, he wasn't in a cold sweat, planning to dash from the classroom with his son in his arms. In fact, he felt a little warm, as if an alarm clock had nudged a dormant memory of sexual attraction.

He smiled wryly. Hallie Ember was one attractive female, but involvement with any woman was out of the question for now. Nate needed all his attention.

The mother near the doorway shuffled forward, awkwardly maintaining her grasp on the collar of her active preschooler, and gave Josh an embarrassed grin. Josh smiled empathetically and returned to his musing. No, the lovely, Hallie Ember with her sun-gold hair and appealing smile was not for him. Sibyl, his ex-wife, hadn't loved him enough to accept him and an asthmatic child. How could another woman?

Josh glanced toward the teacher. Having escorted the latest arrival to a place at the table, Hallie walked across to the harried mother and spoke to her. Josh wondered if she offered the same invitation to stay and observe the children's activities to every parent.

If the invitation was extended, the young mother declined. Glancing quickly at her now occupied son, she balanced the toddler in one arm and prodded the preschooler toward the door with the other hand. Involuntarily, Josh hoped Hallie would move back to his side.

Instead, she glanced at her watch and met her assistant's gaze. Apparently, a changing of the guard or some other momentous occasion loomed in the immediate future. Josh inhaled carefully. Recess?

Unbidden scenes of sumo wrestling between kindergarten-sized opponents, half-mile relay races, and strength-sapping obstacle courses flashed before his eyes. Was this the dreaded recess, where too much exertion on Nate's part could throw him into a full-blown attack in minutes?

Josh nonchalantly slid his hands into the back pockets of his jeans and balanced his weight evenly on his size nines. If Nate glanced his way, he'd see a relaxed, smiling father.

Nothing momentous happened. Youthful hands received a thorough washing, sending a riot of color as eye-catching as Hallie Ember's blouse down the drain. Then the eager students moved on to reading. The teacher read, the students listened. Josh watched in amazement. At home, Nate liked to snuggle close on the sagging sofa and listen to his father read. Now he listened wide-eyed and completely enthralled by the voice of Miss Ember. Josh wasn't surprised. The melodic tone of the teacher's voice made it easy to become entranced.

The song session sounded even better. Hallie Ember should have been on the stage, Josh mused. Beautiful, clear, lilting notes blended with the hodgepodge of youthful voices, bringing them all together—in joy if not in harmony. Josh found himself smiling, almost forgetting his fear of Nate's entrance into alien territory. He pulled his eyes away from the teacher-student group and scanned the surroundings.

The classroom was a large rectangle, furnished with midget-sized tables, chairs, a make-believe kitchen, and a colorful rug. All this and a teacher who made you feel special when her eyes met yours. He glanced at Nate, noting that his wide-eyed attention hadn't waned. He didn't look at the teacher; he looked toward the doorway. What he needed to do was get out of here before he succumbed to her blatant attraction like his son. His decision to leave Nate in the classroom must be based on a teacher's alertness and ability to recognize any symptoms of distress. And, more important, to call him without hesitation.

He found a chair for the rest of the singing session, aware the teacher noted his movement.

He tried to recall what stock he needed to order for the market he owned, or to think about the upcoming repair job for the pier by the lake. He tried *not* to think about what it cost to hire someone to stay in the store while he was at school with Nate. But his nagging thoughts about managing a market and a campground, and rearing an asthmatic child, didn't altogether dispel his awareness of the teacher.

Encouraging the energetic youngsters to form a straight line was much like threading a needle during an earthquake, Hallie decided, reaching out a hand to restrain a wanderer. Finally, amid shuffling feet, jabbing elbows, and shrieking voices, a wobbly line formed. Hallie repressed a sigh of relief and smiled at her assistant bravely. As if it were an everyday occurrence, she stepped back, letting Anna and the children file from the classroom in haphazard chaos.

Once again, she became aware of Josh Snow's presence. He stood up, watching the children file from the room, much as she had.

Despite the anxiety of coping with her new class,

she'd been aware of Josh Snow's attention during the sing-along session. She'd felt his gaze, even though he always seemed to be looking at Nate if she glanced his way. She stopped to straighten a chair in her path before she walked briskly toward him.

"I see you're still with us, Josh. Many parents leave as soon as they see their child is settling in."

Josh grinned. "Then I could have left three minutes after you opened a book, couldn't I?"

Hallie stooped to pick up a sweater, noting the unusual silence in the room. She folded the sweater self-consciously and scanned the floor as if it might be littered with cast-off clothing before she looked up at Josh. "I enjoy reading to children."

"It shows."

"Thank you." Hallie peered at the nametag inside the sweater and walked across the room to place it in the proper box. How could she manage small-talk at a party yet be struck dumb with one amiable father? She crossed to the door. "Are you joining us for recess?"

Josh nodded, standing aside for her to precede him.

Hallie searched for Anna amid the energetic youngsters. Then her gaze darted to the chain-link fence surrounding the area. Assured the gate was closed, she scanned the roller slide that resembled an old-fashioned washboard, the tube slide, and the swings. Both slides and swings abounded with youthful bodies in motion. Nate had commandeered a small red fire truck, and was guiding it slowly along a curved walkway.

She turned to Josh Snow, giving him a confident look. "At least he's trying something a little less strenuous first." She nodded at the youngsters landing on the wood shavings surface beneath the slide and others trotting to claim a swing.

"He's not allergic to red paint as far as I know." His voice was light, but Hallie recognized a note of strain beneath the words.

He must find it difficult being a single parent without the added concerns of a possible asthma attack. She wondered if he had anyone to help him—mother, or housekeeper, or even a girlfriend.

"About food," she said, keeping her gaze on the children. "The school cafeteria sends snacks for the children, and we arrange lunch for those who travel any distance."

"Nate will eat lunch at home and bring his snacks. He can drink the milk here, of course. I want him to fit in with the other students as much as possible."

"Is there a list of foods he can't have?" Hallie hesitated. "I mean, I understand some mothers bring cupcakes for birthdays, and room mothers bake cookies for special occasions. It would be difficult to tell Nate he couldn't participate."

"Those are the little things that keep me awake at night," Josh said wryly.

Empathy touching her, Hallie nodded.

"I'll bring a list of things we know he can eat."

Hallie nodded again. "Anything else to watch for?"

Josh squinted reflectively. "I wouldn't plan on including him in any field trips near smog city."

Hallie grinned, unable to repress a light retort. "Ah, and a school bus trip to the La Brea Tar Pits is one of my fonder memories." She was pleased to see her grin was infectious. Josh's solemn face softened with a smile.

The moment of frivolity was short-lived. A nervous five-year-old approached. Sensing his need, Hallie excused herself and led the youngster toward the rest-room.

She returned to find the smile still lingering on Josh's face. Only this time, he was sharing his son's delight in the muted siren of the fire truck.

"I think Nate likes it here," Josh said as she arrived.

"I'm glad. Mrs. Grant said you might have a few reservations about leaving him."

"I'm not leaving Nate." The pleasant tone of the words was not lessened by the firmness of Joshua Snow's voice.

Hallie managed to keep her mouth closed and her look neutral. Had she misunderstood? She thought Josh Snow had enrolled his son in class. Was the enrollment provisional? He came to check out the class-room, the students, and their teacher before he would trust his son to her care, even for a few hours?

"I mean, Nate is staying, but I'm not leaving."

Hallie lifted an eyebrow quizzically.

"I plan to stay close by."

An inexplicable feeling fluttered across Hallie's chest. Having a single father nearby who doubled his caution to make up for an absent mother caused her some anxiety. Knowing he would stay near the classroom was downright unsettling.

But she nodded agreeably as if the idea sounded perfectly normal. She'd do whatever it took, she told herself, to assure Nathan's enrollment on a permanent basis.

The fire truck, under Nate's youthful guidance, rolled perilously close to Josh's foot, and he stepped aside quickly. Nate turned the steering wheel, and one wheel dropped off the concrete onto the wood shavings. Closer, Hallie reached the truck before Josh, but his hands covered hers as she tugged at the toy fender. He lifted the truck easily, returning the errant wheel to firmer ground.

Hallie sent a confident smile to the accident victim. "The walk seems a little narrower about here, doesn't it?"

Nate looked at her without answering, then concentrated on turning the steering wheel as he pedaled away.

Hallie straightened, aware of the scent of soap and aftershave on the man beside her. She was disturbingly aware that the increased thud of her heart had little to do with the exertion of righting the toy truck.

"I like the way you make kids feel comfortable, even when they goof."

Hallie gazed at the active students. So she was attracted to him. She had little enough time to write after she finished a day in the classroom. She couldn't jeopardize that time by becoming involved with a man. Hadn't the last time taught her anything? "You spend so much time trying to get the ideal man and the ideal romance on paper, you don't have time for the real thing," her fiancé had said as he left.

Besides, the attraction wasn't mutual. His only interest in her was assuring himself she could be trusted to look after his son for a few hours.

Chapter Two

Pine needles crunched beneath Josh's feet as he slowed his steps across the school parking lot to keep pace with his lagging son. The first day of school hadn't harmed Nate as far as Josh could tell. His breathing was normal, and his slow gait was probably reluctance to leave his new classmates and the teacher.

With a teacher like the vivacious Miss Ember, Josh wouldn't have minded staying after school. If he was young and carefree, he added, in admonishment. Now he had a store to manage if he meant to pay tuition for a private school.

Tucking Nate into the passenger seat of his four-wheel-drive, Josh rounded the vehicle and opened the door. He watched with a hint of pride as Nate fastened his seat belt. Nate barely gave him time to slide behind the steering wheel before he asked his usual question.

"Got your belt seat on, Dad?"

Josh restrained a smile. He should correct Nate, but

his son had been reversing the seat-belt thing since he was two. It had become rather endearing.

"Right." He fastened the safety strap methodically for Nate's benefit and checked the side mirrors to see they were focused properly before he pushed the key into the ignition. "Ready for takeoff?"

Nate peered at the dashboard, the door lock, and his taut seat belt. "Ready," he said solemnly.

Josh started the engine and Nate leaned back in his seat as if tired of their game.

Lacy ferns fanned the trunks of firs and pines along the curving road leading down the mountain to the lakeside market. In an opening between the greenery, Josh could see the afternoon sun touching tiers of tree-lined hills and valleys leading to the cities below. Ahead, a long motor home slowed to take a curve, and the driver waved as Josh passed. Returning the wave, Josh rounded the curve and increased his speed. Many of the Labor Day campers had left yesterday. Only those who stretched their holiday outing to the limit might still be in the store.

He glanced at his silent son. "Did you like the school?"

The "yes" Nate uttered was less enthusiastic than Josh had expected. He pursed his lips thoughtfully. It would be easier on him if Josh had a home tutor. He'd had the storage area behind the market remodeled into an all-purpose room soon after he'd leased the market and campground area. Even if he had a sitter, he checked on Nate between customers. So if Nate wasn't thrilled about the school . . . On the other hand, the counselor said Josh needed to be with children his own age.

Josh cleared the next curve adeptly. Maybe he'd overrated Nate's reaction to the attractive teacher and his active classmates. "Did you like the teacher?"

"Uh-huh." Nate gazed at the oncoming traffic.

"I thought she was nice." Josh grinned involuntarily. "Nice" was a mild adjective for what he thought of Hallie Ember. He rounded another curve and wondered briefly if his new clerk, Paul, was having any difficulties with his work at the market. He glanced toward his son. "Did you bring your painting to show Paul?"

"Uh-huh."

Josh felt a familiar twinge of worry. Nate's lack of interest at seeing the wheelchair-bound clerk was unusual. Maybe the classroom activities had tired him. "That's good." His voice showed no hint of his concern, but he risked a second to take his gaze from the road and glance at his son.

Nate rustled the papers clutched in his hand. "Paul makes nicer pictures on his 'puter."

"But yours are original. That's even better." A second glance made Josh breathe easier. Nate's face had brightened.

Two miles later, he turned onto the road leading to the market. Beyond the store, an open gate in the split-rail fencing led to camping spaces for motor homes, campers, tents, and trailers.

Two motor homes, a pickup attached to a fifth-wheeler, and a van occupied the asphalt outside the country store. Inside, the aisles teemed with activity. Half a dozen people talked, laughed, and plopped various items on the counter.

Sending Nate to change into play shorts, Josh hurried to assist Paul with the customers.

With a momentary reprieve, Josh raised an eyebrow at Paul. "More late-leavers than usual."

"One couple's motor home had a balky motor," Paul said. "Their friends waited to get the problem fixed." He turned his head as if he sensed someone waiting. "Hi, Nate, how was school?"

Josh followed Paul's gaze. Nate fidgeted impatiently, paint-smeared pages in hand. When the door closed after the last customer, he rushed forward.

"Paul, look what I did today."

Paul pushed the chair back from the cash register and turned his attention to the animated youngster.

"Hey, now, you didn't tell me you had artistic talents." Paul caught the paper Nate thrust forward.

"I don't have ar . . . art . . . I don't have that. . . ."

"It's not a disease. It's a gift. It means you can draw pretty pictures." Paul scanned the paper solemnly.

"Do you like it?"

"I do."

Nate's face flooded with delight.

Josh turned to the meat slicer, wiping the machine with more vigor than care.

"How do you like your teacher?" Paul asked.

Josh glanced at Nate, seeing him tilt his head and squint his eyes in childish concentration. "She's good at reading books and singing. She's pretty, too"

"Aha." Paul ruffled Nate's fair hair. "Must be a pretty special teacher. Does this mean you'd like to go to her class every day?"

Nate's eyes flared with animation. "Yeah," he said enthusiastically. "We get to line up and go outside and play. It's called . . ." His small forehead wrinkled, and he squinted fiercely before looking to his father for help with the unfamiliar word.

Josh kept a straight face. "Recess."

The wrinkles disappeared, the eyes widened, and Nate grinned broadly at Paul. "Recess," he repeated succinctly.

Josh felt a twinge of jealousy. He gave Nate every moment of his day . . . and night, more or less. And Nate had barely spoken to him about his day at school.

Josh eyed the slicer, scanning the shiny surface for a speck of soil. Having lost his own son in the accident that killed his wife, Paul doted on Nate. Wasn't it natural for Nate to respond? Josh pushed the slicer back in place. He tried to spend time with Nate—quality time, like he'd read in some parenting book—but his first concern was Nate's health. His second was keeping a roof over his son's head, food in his mouth, and enough money in the bank to pay his medical bills. How could a five-year-old compare that to playing with Paul and his computer? He looked up, realizing his son was looking at him.

"I'm thirsty."

Josh grinned. When it came to the basics . . . "Chocolate milk in the cooler." His son ambled over to the glass-doored cooler, and Josh watched him with parental fondness, plus a touch of relief. Nate had been among strangers in a new environment this afternoon. Paints and carpets, wood shavings, and heaven knew what else in the pockets of his classmates. Yet there was no evidence of respiratory distress in his impish face.

Josh turned to Paul. "Busy day?" For the first time since he'd entered the store, he really looked at his temporary employee. The usual week-old stubble was missing, exposing a fairly good-looking face, despite the gaunt cheeks.

Paul scrubbed his freshly shaved chin self-consciously. "Busy right after you left, as you predicted. But if it hadn't been for the mishap that caused the last bunch to leave later, I'd have been wheeling around here with nothing to do."

Josh laughed. "There's never 'nothing to do' in a country market."

"Right." Paul joined in the laughter. "But I couldn't find the feather duster."

"I appreciate your taking over today."

Paul raised his shoulders, rotating one before he lowered it self-consciously. "It was great to have something to do."

"Think you'd consider working weekday afternoons?"

"You've decided to enroll Nate in school, then?"

Josh looked toward Nate, seeing he'd mastered opening the carton. "Sounds like I have little choice, doesn't it?"

Paul nodded. "With a teacher who reads books,

sings, and is pretty to boot, you might have trouble convincing Nate that home is better."

"Right," Josh said, trying not to think about the teacher. "Which poses a problem. I can't leave Nate with a stranger, even for a few hours, nor can I afford to close the store. So if you think you can handle it, the job's yours." Remorse stabbed Josh at his choice of words. But from the grin on Paul's face, no offense had been taken.

"I guess all I need is a time card."

Josh released his breath. Keeping the store open wasn't as important as being with Nate, but closing it, even for a few hours, would lessen his income. "Good."

Paul held up one hand, palm out. "But you'll have to put the jam, pickles, mayo, and other things in jars on lower shelves if I'm going to stock."

Josh laughed in relief. "Is that all? I'll replenish the shelves mornings and weekends. So, I'll see you at noon tomorrow."

"Noon tomorrow." Paul wheeled his chair around the counter. "Have a good day at school."

Josh lifted his eyebrows in feigned hopelessness, pantomiming that the mere thought of enjoying the return to a classroom filled with exuberant kindergartners was ludicrous. The unusual feeling in his chest further belied the gesture.

Hallie saw two afternoon students enter the classroom before she lowered her gaze to look for the missing crayons. She'd worked on a new script until after eleven last night, erasing whole paragraphs on the monitor screen more often than saving them. She hadn't had a restful night, and the morning session of her kindergarten class had been a replay of the chaos of yesterday. She looked forward to greeting the afternoon students with mixed feelings.

Supporting her weight on one knee, she ducked beneath the table to retrieve another rolling crayon and heard the door open again. Despite a glance at the clock on the wall, which told her less than three minutes had passed, she knew she'd been chasing the array of colors for at least ten minutes, looking up expectantly each time the door opened. She felt a vague sense of disappointment as a ponytailed moppet entered the room. She bent to look for another crayon. She wasn't looking forward to seeing Nate Snow any more than she was the rest of the children, she told herself. Well, maybe a little more. Twenty or so hours ago, when Josh and Nate had left the classroom, there still seemed to be a question about Nate's return. That, surely, was the cause of her anxiety. Nate's father might have decided against leaving him in her care.

She'd thought they both left in good spirits. She'd tried to see that Nate enjoyed school without singling him out; she'd tried to show his father, without pressuring him, that Nate would do well in her classroom. She told herself that Mrs. Grant needed every student she could enroll in the private school. She'd told herself a lot of things between intermittent thoughts about the father and son.

On arising this morning, the pair had again rambled

through her consciousness. She'd changed clothes twice for no reason she could rationalize. She'd finally donned walking shorts and a blouse and still arrived in her classroom earlier than required. She'd cut out far too many paper animals for a class project, then spilled a jar of red paint on half of them. When the morning students arrived, she found her ability to coax the noisy, energetic youngsters into a straight line hadn't improved, and she wondered if she'd brought any aspirin with her.

The start of the afternoon session didn't go well, either. Anna, her assistant, had left hurriedly after receiving a call that her mother had been injured in an accident. The principal, Lydia Grant, had arrived to help, but the exuberant youngsters strained even *her* patience. Hallie had spilled the crayons in her haste to look prepared and nonchalant when the door opened for her afternoon students.

Pulling her head back from beneath the table, she lifted it slightly and peered over the tabletop. Josh stood in the doorway, silhouetted against the bright noonday sun. He looked bigger than she remembered— just under six feet, with broad shoulders that filled the space inside the door frame. His muscular legs were encased in close-fitting jeans today, and a blue T-shirt stretched across his chest. Nate had preceded him into the room, dashing across to the box she'd shown him the day before, as if making sure she hadn't removed his name.

Josh moved his head, his gaze following his son, and the sunlight struck shafts of gold in his auburn hair. She couldn't pull her gaze away as he stepped into the room. As he did yesterday, he scanned the room closely, his gaze pausing on the principal, who was helping a student remove her backpack. A perplexed frown creased his face. Then he looked back toward Nate. Another student moved toward Nate, and Josh's face changed. The change was subtle, but maybe she could detect the wariness because she knew of the father's anxiety.

She knew what worried him, but what had caused it? The child approaching Nate was just another towheaded kindergartner carrying a shoebox. His show-and-tell presentation, no doubt. Then it dawned on her that Josh would be cautious of any new animal, plant, or food that might come in contact with his son. She pushed herself to her feet and crossed the room, reaching the two boys a step ahead of Josh, but a second too late to prevent the opening of the box. She caught a glimpse of the small, white rat inside and raised her gaze to look at Josh. She hadn't expected the grin she saw on his face.

"Nate has a white rat."

She nodded, breathing carefully so her voice wouldn't come in gasps. "Robby volunteered to bring a show-and-tell today." She smiled at the youngster. "Maybe you should cover your pet for now. You don't want him to get nervous with all the people around." She waited until the boxtop was replaced, then suggested Robby place the box on the teacher's desk until showtime.

Realizing she still carried the crayon in her hand,

she shoved it in the pocket of her walking shorts as the principal approached.

"Hallie, I must get back to the office. I have an appointment. Our secretary is calling for a temp to assist you, but it may not be this afternoon." She crossed the room and stopped before she reached the doorway, turning back to Hallie. "Will you be okay?"

Hallie smiled. "I'll be fine."

Lydia Grant smiled, but Hallie could tell her attention had already left the room and was probably half-way to the school office, if not already in silent conversation with her "appointment." But she wasn't surprised when Mrs. Grant took time to speak to Josh before she hurried through the doorway. The older teacher was a diplomat.

Josh looked at Hallie after the principal's departure, then crossed the few steps separating them. "Problem?" His eyes sparked with concern.

"Nothing to do with the children," Hallie hastened to assure him.

"Are you sure?" His gaze sought out his son, as if a miniature airborne alien might be circling the room.

Hallie's gaze followed his look with a touch of compassion. Of course any change in the classroom routine would cause Josh anxiety. She'd thought he was going to leap across the classroom and rescue Nate from the breath of the monster in Robby's shoe-box.

"It's only a problem for me . . . for this afternoon." She smiled, reassuring the anxious father again. "My assistant was called away. Her mother was in a car accident."

"Oh." Josh flushed. "I'm sorry. Somehow, I relate everything to me. Or to how it will affect Nate. I know it sounds selfish." He took a breath. "I'm sorry about your assistant. Maybe I can help."

His offer touched Hallie. He wasn't as selfish as he thought if he could offer his help to others, even while he worried about his son. "The school secretary is calling for a temp, but she probably can't get one soon enough to help today."

Josh raised one hand, his face comically serious, to smooth an errant lock of hair back from his forehead. He used both hands to smooth the neck of his T-shirt before lowering them and straightening his spine. "I have a Master's degree in business"—the comic face slipped and a wry grin replaced it—"which is little recommendation for corralling kindergartners. But I'm a quick study, and I'm willing to learn."

Hallie grinned.

"I can give you references. And I must be good with kids. Nate likes me." He grinned.

He can smile, Hallie thought. He was different when he smiled. His face relaxed, and the crease lines of the smile eradicated his usual wariness. He must work the late shift, or maybe nights, she mused. "It wouldn't interfere with your current employment?" she asked. Then she felt like a fool. He lived in a campground. Maybe he didn't have a job.

Josh didn't seem to notice her embarrassment. "I can manage."

Hallie hesitated. What would Mrs. Grant say? She didn't know if parents were allowed to work in the same classroom with their children.

"I'll be underfoot here anyway." Josh looked up as another student entered, then left Hallie's side and went to help the youngster remove his backpack and store it in the allocated bin. He returned, a new smile building. "How's that for on-the-job training?"

"I'm impressed. But you'll need to talk to the principal. I don't know if she hires parents as temps."

"I wasn't thinking about being a temp. I was volunteering."

"Even better for the school, I'd think, financially. But you still need to see Mrs. Grant, and you may need to fill in a form for volunteers." She pursed her lips. "Don't tell the kindergartners, but teaching here is new to me. I'm still learning the ropes."

"We can learn together."

"Sounds interesting." Hallie smiled broadly. In more ways than one, she thought.

"It does," Josh agreed.

"What do we do first?"

Hallie blinked. The "we" part of his question sounded nice. But she knew not to make too much of it. She gave her new volunteer a friendly grin and lifted a slender hand to encompass the milling students in the classroom. "Believe it or not, we spend a big share of our time trying to get the children in lines."

"Lines?" Josh's look questioned her seriousness.

Hallie's eyes sparkled mischievously. She was beginning to enjoy this kindergarten-teaching thing.

"Lines. It's one way to establish a minimal degree of order." She motioned at the active students. "One teacher I met delights in bemoaning the fact that she needed a college education in order to spend three-fourths of the school year teaching kindergartners to line up or sit down."

Josh chuckled. "I didn't notice you having any difficulty yesterday."

"You were late and missed the fun." Her smile broadened. "I dreaded getting the kids to sit without Anna's help. So here's your chance to show off your expertise in the management part of your business education."

"Besides my business partner, our company had four employees. My partner and I took turns making, marketing, and delivering our wares, right along with our employees."

Hallie snagged a kindergartner on his way to the door. "It isn't recess time yet," she said mildly. Guiding him toward the table, she glanced at Josh. He owned a business and lived in a campground? "Is your business near here?"

"Not that business. The smog in the city was bad for Nate, so I sold it to my partner in order to move to the mountains. I leased a country store with a camping area near the lake. Business isn't as good, but I can spend more time with Nate, and his health has improved. That's the important thing."

A wave of admiration washed across Hallie, leaving a tickle of sand in her throat that clogged any words she might have uttered, even if she could think of something to say. Fortunately, Josh was turning away, his attention focused on the energetic students. He sidestepped to prevent a backpack-laden speeder from rear-ending an unsuspecting dawdler with effortless ease. Then he straightened and turned back to Hallie.

"As to finding the secret of Anna's success, let's think positive. Are we going to let five-year-olds defeat us?"

Minutes later, Hallie wondered if her volunteer would resign before the class even started. She looked aside warily. Josh Snow, with a set smile on his face, was firmly guiding each child to a chair. She took a breath and caught a shaggy-haired, shorts-clad youngster imitating a marathon racer. Josh might or might not have the right technique for calming five-year-olds, but she couldn't argue with the results.

Somehow she made it through the first session and looked forward to recess.

Which was no better. A pretty, blond ponytailed youngster fell and skinned a knee, and Josh took her to the office to see the school nurse. One boy pushed another, and a wailing match ensued. By the time recess was over and Hallie had maneuvered the youngsters toward an already wobbly lineup, she doubted she'd made any points with Nate's father. If he was looking for an efficient, organized teacher to whom he could entrust his son for a few hours, she'd blown it.

Coaxing two reluctant boys from the seesaw, Josh glanced toward Hallie with admiration. How she kept up with the youngsters was a marvel. She'd separated two miniature brawlers with more ease than a bouncer in a beer hall and handled the sight of blood with the stoic demeanor of an emergency room nurse. True, blood was barely visible on the scraped skin of the ponytailed child who had fallen, but his breath caught in his chest as he imagined what would happen if Nate even stumbled. He'd noticed her indecision on whether to take the child to the nurse or stay with the remaining children. He was glad she decided to stay, since he didn't relish the thought of being left alone with a dozen or so rampant bodies in search of an accident—any more than he did accompanying the injured child, he thought wryly. But he'd been brave. He hadn't panicked. He'd been determined to accept her decision. He'd taken the tiny hand of the teary-eyed child and comforted her with the thought of funny-face bandages awaiting her. He'd even managed to leave the schoolyard without stopping to assure himself that Nate was sound of limb and wind.

His gaze roved over the schoolyard placidly. Maybe he had made the right decision to enroll Nate in the class. Hallie Ember seemed to have rotating radar equipment installed on top of her head that detected any child's need for attention. Her reactions were calm, caring, and responsible.

Of course, he'd be less than a hundred feet away with a mobile phone and beeper in hand. Hallie Ember could call him anytime. Involuntarily, a grin tugged at his lips. Once that thought would have contained another meaning. He shrugged the thought away roughly and turned to assist the teacher as she cheerfully attempted to interest the children in returning to the classroom in an orderly fashion.

Chapter Three

With the Thursday morning class entrusted to their caretakers, Hallie longed for a lunch break, something she hadn't managed for almost a week. The temp had arrived last Friday, making Josh's volunteer position superfluous—an unidentifiable disappointment. The same temp returned on Monday, Tuesday, Wednesday, and today. The young woman was helpful, but she wasn't Anna. Or Josh.

The last lingering student trudged out the open door and involuntarily Hallie's gaze went to the parking lot, searching for Josh's four-wheeler. After volunteer duty last week, Josh had seemed withdrawn. He'd arrived as usual with Nate on Monday, said hello in a friendly fashion, and left until it was time to pick up his son. She'd spoken in the same friendly manner and wondered if she'd upset him. She noted his problem didn't interfere with his jogging past the school, his beeper barely visible above the edge of his T-shirt pocket. Her wondering, however, had been interfering with her writing.

Hallie closed the door, walked to the teacher's lounge, and retrieved her sack lunch. She popped the lid on the cola can, took a sip, and dropped onto a plastic-covered chair as the door opened again.

"Hi, Midge," she greeted a co-worker.

The dark-haired woman smiled. "Hoped I'd catch you sometime today." Like Hallie had just done, she walked to the fridge and removed a sack lunch. The young woman sat opposite Hallie and took a fat sandwich from the recesses of her bag. "I looked for you yesterday."

"Yesterday was a bit chaotic."

"What day isn't?" The teacher peeled plastic wrap from tan-colored bread.

Hallie pulled the peanut butter and cracker package from her bag. "You wanted to see me?"

Midge swallowed and took a moment to clear her throat. "I wanted to invite you to a barbecue this weekend. I'll even supply a tall, dark, handsome hunk." She grinned. "He's not exactly tall, but he does have mischievous brown eyes to die for."

Hallie thought of Josh's deep blue eyes—often solemn, but glowing with love when he looked at his son. She wondered if he'd looked at his wife that way. "Brown eyes are nice." Her attempt to be polite made her reply sound vague.

"Oops." The teacher hesitated. "I should have asked if you're engaged or something. But I didn't notice a ring on your finger." She looked at Hallie warily. "Are you?"

Hallie chuckled wryly, pausing in her attempt to pierce at the plastic protection around the crackers. "Not engaged. Not even 'or something.' My last romantic involvement came to a rather sudden end when a role in a Broadway-bound play was offered to my boyfriend."

Midge looked sympathetic. "Why didn't you go with him?"

"He didn't ask me." Instead of the gloom that would have once accompanied the answer, Hallie's voice was upbeat, with a hint of self-deprecating humor. "Between stuffing his belongings into a duffle bag, calling his agent, his trainer, and his mother, my once-significant other informed me I was a poor romantic risk, or words to that effect."

"Sour grapes?"

Hallie shook her head. "He might have been right. He said I spent too much time writing."

"Men do need attention."

"We went places together, when he wasn't at an acting class or an audition. He lived across the hall and was in and out of my place all the time. But he said my fingers were always attached to the computer keyboard and my mind was in another world."

"Men," Midge said compassionately.

Hallie shrugged. Perhaps she'd overdone the computer time. Or maybe they weren't right for each other and it was just her ego that was hurt. Her sense of rejection again. She found a weak spot in the plastic and ripped the wrapper open as if a clue to her feelings hovered inside.

"I hope that doesn't mean you're off men for life," Midge teased.

Hallie eyed the crumbling crackers dubiously. "No." She thought of the blue-eyed father of one of her students. "I wish I could say yes to your invitation. But a friend in Los Angeles—to be more precise, Studio City—is expecting me to arrive Friday evening and stay the weekend." She separated the crackers.

"Maybe another time," Midge said. She peered into her bag and withdrew a carton of pudding.

"Maybe."

Two more teachers entered the lounge. The conversation turned to food and clothes and weather, as if they had already been invited to the barbecue. The crackers consumed, Hallie withdrew a yogurt cup from her bag. The invitation was nice. But going to Los Angeles to meet the writer's group was more important. She had to remember her priorities. Time away from her day job meant writing, or talking about writing, or thinking about writing. Selling a script was her ticket to acceptance, wasn't it?

She slid a spoonful of yogurt into her mouth. She hadn't heard anything about the optioned script. She knew her agent had her new number; she'd called his secretary twice, once leaving the number of the school, and she checked daily with the school secretary and Lydia's answering machine. He hadn't called, which wasn't new. She'd been waiting for *the* call for years.

She sighed. Alex was a nice guy. He praised her

writing, modestly. He returned her telephone calls when he had nothing positive to report. From what her fellow writers said, he was a good agent. But even a call from his secretary to say that the script was still in the running, or that someone was interested in one of her other projects, would be nice. She scraped the last of the yogurt from the carton and told herself she would *not* stop by the office to telephone him on the way to her afternoon class. Calling him too often wasn't cool.

She cradled the empty carton dreamily. When one of her scripts had been optioned almost a year ago, she thought she had it made. That was until a pro, five years older but decades wiser about the business of writing, told her that while dozens of screenplays were optioned, few were bought.

"What?" Hallie turned at the sound of her name.

"Room mother," the speaker replied.

"Room mother?" Hallie wrinkled her forehead.

"Do you have a room mother for your room yet?"

Room mother. Hallie focused on the words. Oh, yes . . . that was one of those things on her to-do list. She'd sent notices with her students, doubting that a dozen eager parents would rush in vying for the honor. Since no one offered, her days of continuing crisis had relegated the matter to a "tomorrow" category.

Hallie recapped her empty yogurt cup. "I'm working on it."

Midge laughed. "Better work fast, if your class schedule is anything like mine. We're going on a field trip next week, and I still need all the help I can beg, bribe, or coerce with guilt feelings. This is my second year, but I can remember how cowardly I felt at leaving the security of the classroom with my unpredictable horde."

Laughter filled the room followed by another teacher's account of her nightmare field trip.

A room mother. Most of the parents greeted her hurriedly before urging a dawdling child forward as if they were double-parked on a city street.

Conversation stalled as the school secretary entered and the teachers greeted her. Returning the greeting, she waved a note toward Hallie as she spoke to another teacher. For a moment, Hallie forgot the room mother problem. Hope flickered in her chest. Maybe, just maybe, her agent had finally called. She waited impatiently for the secretary to turn from the other teacher. She even tried not to look too expectant.

"Hallie." The secretary's tone was teasing. "Don't know if you call this good news or bad news."

Hallie took a short breath. So what if the secretary remembered Hallie had pestered her about a call from her agent and felt she deserved teasing. So what if the news wasn't what she wanted. At least her agent had called.

"Two less two-legged terrors in your classroom this afternoon." The secretary extended the note.

Hallie reached for the slip, her mind trying to shift gears without shifting her facial expression. Just the names of children whose parents had called. She stilled her disappointment. Crumpling her lunch bag, she excused herself from the other teachers.

She didn't retrieve the note from her desk where she'd tossed it until the new aide settled the children on the "magic carpet," as they'd renamed the colorful rug.

Nate Snow's was the second name scrawled in the secretary's now familiar handwriting.

Hallie glanced at the students on the carpet as if the note could be wrong. She'd been disappointed, but not worried when Nate and his father had been absent yesterday. But again today?

She frowned. Nate had used his hand-held inhaler intermittently during class on Tuesday, but he'd used it before and still came to school the next day. Josh was probably being cautious, she told herself.

Her concern over Nate's absence popped up again while she washed paint-stained hands and turned pages in a book. It continued as she helped departing students with their backpacks and waved to parents. It came up again when she sat down to write. Maybe she should call Josh. If something Nate came in contact with in the classroom had caused his problem, she should be aware of it, to guard against future problems. But if she stopped working now, she knew how easy it was to forgo writing. She turned on the computer.

In her story, Cindy Ellen was a limo driver, and Prince Charming was a successful attorney who'd hired the services of the limo for the weekend. Sparks were already beginning to fly. Fantasyland wasn't far away for both Cindy Ellen and Hallie. The real world was on hold.

On Friday morning, Hallie took the note off the door to her classroom and tucked it into her palm without glancing at it. Her mind was on Cindy Ellen's current dilemma. She looked at the orderly room and came back to earth. In half an hour, clutter, chaos, and chatter would reign. Then she smiled. In eight hours or so, she'd be on her way down the mountain and on the freeway to the city. A few hours after that she'd be amid the writing group, catching up on the latest market news and industry gossip. She dropped the note on the desk with her armload of papers, stored her purse, and slipped off her light jacket.

The tune escaping her throat and echoing in the empty classroom lasted until she returned to the desk and opened the note. The tune ended rather abruptly.

Nate was on the absentee list again.

Early arriving youngsters gave her little time to muse over the information. She put the note aside and moved to greet the boys.

Later, watching a wobbly line of kindergartners leave the classroom for the playground, she wondered if she should visit her ailing student. She scoffed at her mental question. If teachers visited every child who was out because of illness, they'd never get their own homework done. She followed the children to the play area.

She could say she was driving to see a friend and saw the campground and thought she'd stop by since she was in the area. Or she was out of milk. Josh had said he managed a country store, didn't he? She restrained a giggle and moved rapidly to deter a youngster from a daring escape over the chain-link fence, reminding herself she going to the city as soon as she left class and packed her overnight bag.

On moving to the mountains, she'd promised her agent she'd be in Hollywood on weekends. She'd called her writing friend and accepted her standing invitation. On weekends, her priority was her writing career.

But by the time she'd found the last backpack, hugged the last child, and straightened the classroom, she was vacillating between visiting Nate and not visiting Nate. She retrieved her purse and looked up as the door opened.

The school principal stood in the open doorway. "Hallie, I know you're anxious to get on the road to L.A. Still, I thought I'd invite you to an impromptu meeting with the other teachers, sort of to discuss how the first two weeks have gone."

Hallie restrained a grimace. She wanted to be in the city in time to go to dinner with the group, and she knew, unconsciously, she'd decided to stop and see Nate before she got on the freeway. Yet she needed all the input anyone offered on classroom activities, even if her plans to stay at the mountain school were limited.

"Thanks, Lydia. I'll be there."

It was five by the time the meeting broke up. Hallie waved to the others in departure, her mind already on her forthcoming trip. Traffic on the freeway wasn't bad going into Los Angeles this time of day, but she still had to change and pick up her overnight bag. Maybe she'd skip seeing Nate.

It wasn't quite six when she placed the bag in her car and started down the mountain. She didn't have time to find the campground and visit Nate and his father. But if she didn't, an inner voice nagged, she'd worry all weekend. She'd casually mentioned to Lydia that Nate Snow had been absent lately, and asked about the campground where he lived.

"I think it's called Whispering Firs," Lydia had said after a reflective stare. "I've noticed the turnoff sign on the road."

Hallie braked for a slow-moving car. The place couldn't be too far away, and she would only stay a few minutes. She could still be in Los Angeles by nine. Besides, she'd thought of a legitimate reason to stop by the store. She needed a room mother, or rather, a room *dad*.

Glancing through the window on the left side of the store entrance, Josh scanned the sunny but empty parking lot. Morning shoppers had come and gone, as had the afternoon browsers, so he should have an hour to stock the shelves before the influx of Friday campers. He turned and walked to the back room, pausing to glance around the partition that separated the storeroom from Nate's playroom. His plate half full, Nate was engrossed in the televised travels of a canine adventurer. Relieved, Josh watched his son for a moment before proceeding to the stacked boxes.

His position as a volunteer aide had been short-lived. Nathan's lethargy on Tuesday developed into sniffles on Wednesday. With the possibility of a cold looming on his son's horizon, Josh was jolted into remembering why he could have no life of his own— even one limited to spending a few hours volunteering in a position where Nate was with him. He'd enjoyed being near Nate's teacher, even in the company of the noisy, energetic youngsters. The fantasy of a future in volunteering slipped past the barriers of his problems. Reality set in when he noticed Nate's use of his inhaler.

He paused, listening for the sound of the bell over the entry doors. Paul should be returning soon. He'd helped most of the day, staying in the store while Josh fixed Nate's meals or reading to Nate when Josh brought him down to the playroom. At five, Paul had left Nate eating dinner in front of the TV and crossed the short distance to eat with his parents.

Hearing no sound, Josh bent to pick up a carton of beef stew, carried it to a nearly depleted shelf, and deftly opened the box. Beef stew was a good seller. Though with crockpots simmering, awaiting the arrival of fishermen who'd been on the lake for hours, not to mention minute-ready microwave dinners, it was a surprise anyone opened a can these days. Half the carton was empty when the double doors of the store opened. Straightening his back, Josh smiled a welcome.

Paula, Paul's mother, shouldered one double door open and pushed the other aside with her empty hand. Paul wheeled inside, and Josh was reminded that he meant to look into the cost of installing automatic doors.

"You didn't rest long," Josh admonished.

Paul made a face. "I couldn't find Nate's newest tape, so I left him watching that dog film. It's ancient and he's seen it a zillion times, so I was afraid he'd gobble dinner and get restless."

"Discounting a fishing trip," Josh said, his laughter belying the resigned look he directed toward the ceiling, "that tape is good for a zillion and one reruns. It's the second copy I've bought." He grinned as Paula lowered the covered plate to the counter. "Smells delicious."

"Roast beef, vegetables, and deep dish apple pie for dessert."

Josh shook his head in gentle protest. "I have shelves of food." He glanced at the canned beef stew and put it aside before he walked to meet Paula.

"I've seen what you eat. How healthy are potato chips and a slice of whatever cold cut is available?"

Josh chuckled. "I take vitamins. What else do I need?"

Paula wrinkled her brow. "What you need is a wife. She might even encourage you to take an hour off occasionally."

"I take off every afternoon, almost."

"From the store, maybe. But not from watching Nate."

"I don't watch him every minute. I have some help," Josh retorted humorously.

Paula grinned broadly. "I've heard about your help. And I hear Nate is very taken with his teacher."

"He isn't reluctant to go to school."

"Married or engaged?" Paula asked.

Josh took a breath, lifted his eyes toward the ceiling, and anticipated Paula's next teasing remark.

"Maybe you should find out if she's *available*," Paula said as if on cue, emphasizing the word with a broad grin, "before someone else shows her the attractions of our mountains." Without waiting for a comment, she nodded at the food. "Eat before it gets cold. I've got to get back and finish the dishes before my TV program starts."

"Thanks for the dinner," Josh called to her departing back.

Paul looked toward the shelves Josh had been refilling. "I'll finish stocking if you want to go in back and relax with your dinner."

"No, I'll eat here." Josh walked behind the counter and pulled a stool up to a low shelf big enough to hold a plate and a coffee cup. He had a sliver of roast beef on the way to his mouth when Paul spoke.

"Mom means no harm," Paul said quietly. "She just thinks marriage is the end of the rainbow."

Josh slid the beef in his mouth and chewed slowly. Once he'd thought marriage was the end of the rainbow. He wanted to be married. He wanted a wife and children and the smell of something baking in the oven or simmering on the stove when he came in from work. His parents had been good role models. Until he was fourteen, he thought every mother smelled of vanilla and wore tennis shoes and walking shorts summer and winter. His mother had been killed in a plane accident before she saw her first grandchild, and his father had seen Nate only once. He'd been transferred to Africa to open a new branch of the bank where he worked. Since his remarriage and the responsibilities of his new position, communication had dwindled to one call a month.

Paul's quiet laughter spread across the store. "Better her matchmaking is aimed at you than me. And Nate's teacher sounds pretty great."

Josh swallowed and took a sip of cola. "Paula needn't play cupid in that direction. Hallie Ember is here as a substitute teacher. I can't see her settling down in a small mountain community with a ready-made family." A family that came with problems he couldn't ask her to face. The thought zoomed through Josh's mind like a sandstorm, grating the sound in his throat. He glanced at Paul quickly, hoping he hadn't heard the bitter note in his voice.

But Paul was testing the brake on his wheelchair. "I would like to meet the lady. From Nate's description, she's pretty, kind, and loves children."

"She is all that." Josh bent his head, studying the colorful array of peas and carrots on his plate.

"Then why don't you ask her out?"

Josh grinned wryly. "I suppose I could carry Nate and his inhaler in a backpack when I trudge up to her front door. Shouldn't put a damper on dinner, should it?"

"Not if she's as nice as Nate says," Paul said cheerfully.

Josh concentrated on connecting a baby carrot to a fork tine. Paul knew the problems he had with Nate's health, but he hadn't discussed his other problem with anyone after Sibyl left. It wasn't exactly easy conversation.

"I could stay with Nate, you know." Paul wheeled his chair toward the back room. "Let me know when." He left the phrase as if he expected Josh to pick up the telephone and dial Hallie's number.

"Don't hold your breath," Josh said in a low voice. He looked at the deep-dish apple pie. "If I knew she could cook like your mother—" he managed to make his voice as cheery as his employee's—"I might look up her telephone number."

"Coward," Paul called back.

Josh shook his head. Paul was more a friend than an employee these days. Still, he didn't confide his personal problem easily. And what was the need? His situation couldn't be changed.

He was relieved when the bell sounded over the door again. He smiled broadly, slipping a half-empty plate under the counter and greeted the prospective shoppers with more enthusiasm than usual. The Andersons didn't usually shop for their weekend supplies until they reached the campground, which increased Josh's cash flow.

Another influx of shoppers arrived and left, and Josh looked in to find Nate asleep on the couch and Paul engrossed in his program. He grinned and returned to stocking the shelves. Aligning another can on the shelf, he though of Hallie. She was so different from Sibyl. It was evident she enjoyed being with children, in the smile that engulfed her eyes, in the lilt of her voice as she knelt on one knee to speak to them, in the spontaneous hugs she dispensed at random. He was relieved when the sound of the door opening interrupted his thoughts before they went further.

Hallie found the campground easily. Beyond the grove of pines and firs mingled between the campsites, the lake glowed in the setting sun. She turned onto the asphalt-covered parking lot surrounding three sides of a two-story log-sided building. A brown and white MARKET sign loomed above the doorway.

A small bell sounded as she opened and closed the door. Then there was silence. She scanned the neatly stocked shelves, the polished glass of the display cases, and the empty aisles. She clutched her car keys tightly, her mind tumbling. What was she doing here? She could have called Josh to inquire about Nate's health. She could still call from Los Angeles. A slight noise—like an exhaled breath—sounded, and she turned. Josh's head rose above a large carton, and his face broke into a smile that swept her indecisive thoughts away.

"Hi." She felt floaty and foolish and disorganized.

"Hi." He lowered the box and shoved it aside with his foot. "I thought about closing so I could finish replenishing the shelves. I'm glad I didn't. Something I can help you with?"

"I'm glad you didn't close too." Hallie stared at a nearby display, vaguely noting the cereal labels. "Milk. I need milk for my cereal in the morning."

"And this was the nearest market?" Josh's eyes twinkled.

"Not exactly. I wanted to check on Nate. And to ask you a favor. First, how is Nate?"

"Good. I think he'll be back in school Monday. His red eyes and sniffling have cleared, and he's gettin' bored. Paul, a friend, is with him in what we call the rec room. I think he's asleep." Josh grinned apologetically. "Give me a minute to hang out the closed sign and lock the door, and we'll go see him." He moved toward the front doors.

"I don't want you to wake him."

Josh chortled, moving back to her side. "Not wake him! I couldn't live on the same planet with him if he found out you were here and I let him sleep."

A flush of pleasure rippled through Hallie. "I wouldn't want to be responsible for your move to Mars."

"This way, then." Josh walked down the aisle to a doorway closed with a vertical blind. Drawing it aside, he waited for Hallie to enter.

The large space inside had been partitioned, with cartons and crates on one side and a small cozy room on the other. A young man near Josh's age sat in a wheelchair, watching a lighted television screen. On a nearby couch, Nate slept on his back with one small arm flung toward his tousled hair.

The young man looked up at their entry and pressed

a button on the remote control he held. The sounds from the set waned.

"Hallie, this is Paul, my friend who helps me in the store while I'm with Nate at school."

Paul straightened in his chair and leaned forward to extend a hand. "Nate's teacher. I'd recognize you any-where, well, almost anywhere, from Josh . . ."—he paused imperceptibly—"and Nate's descriptions of you. I'm glad to meet you. Are you searching for tru-ants?"

"Miss Ember was concerned about Nate's continued absence from the classroom," Josh said gruffly.

Returning Paul's friendly smile, Hallie felt Paul's hand clasp hers in a firm grip. "Josh and Nate ne-glected to tell me about you, but I'm glad to meet you too." She withdrew her hand.

Paul's laughter rippled over the room. "It might sound a little odd for Josh to tell people he had a new clerk with gorgeous hair and great legs."

Hallie felt her cheeks flush.

"I didn't say that," Josh sputtered.

"Not exactly." Paul raised one hand and waggled it from side to side.

Josh cleared his throat. "I hate to wake Nate, but you know he won't like it if he hears Hallie was here and he didn't see her." He crossed the room and shook his son's shoulder gently. Nate grunted softly and turned over, tossing his arm over his chest.

"Let him sleep a little longer," Paul suggested. "You can take a breather. You haven't been out of the store all day."

Josh looked at his son for a minute before turning to Hallie. "Do you have time for a cup of coffee or tea?"

Hallie shook her head. "Not really."

Paul interrupted. "I meant, get some fresh air. Show Miss Ember the lake. I'll stay with Nate. I'd like to see the end of the program on TV anyway."

Hallie turned toward Paul. "Call me Hallie. And I'd like to see the lake, but I'm on my way to Los Angeles."

"What's more important in Los Angeles than a view of our lake in the moonlight?"

"For me, networking. I'm on my way to Studio City, actually. My agent says it's important to circulate, see and be seen, and learn what story line is hot this year."

"You're a writer?" Paul said.

"A writer, not a seller." She paused dramatically and grinned in humorous self-deprecation. "Yet."

"So why are you teaching in the mountains?"

"A writer needs to eat. I'm only subbing for a few months."

"I'm sure some of us will hate to see you go." Paul grinned, and Hallie glanced involuntarily at Josh, aware he listened without comment.

Bidding Paul good-night, Hallie preceded Josh through the open doorway, wondering if he would be among those who hated to see her go.

She stepped outside into the dusky evening, her steps heavy with reluctance, and walked toward her car. Josh slowed to keep in step with her, his body brushing against hers, and the reluctance increased. She forced her feet to improve their pace. She would be late enough getting to the city as it was.

Josh stepped forward and reached for the car door handle, but he didn't open the door, as if he too, was reluctant to end their meeting. "The lake is beautiful after the sun goes down. Most of the fishermen are in, and the campers and children are having dinner, so it's quiet and peaceful."

The scent of his aftershave floated toward Hallie, and pine needles rustled nearby. Farther away, a shimmer of light splashed the surface of the lake, and there was a sound of something that might be the hull of a boat bumping a wooden dock. Overhead, a high-pressure sodium light crackled and flickered to life, breaking the momentary silence between them.

Josh made a sound in his throat. "You wanted to ask me a favor?"

Hallie stared at him, her senses still tuned to the tangy aroma of aftershave and pine trees, of lapping water and soft dusky skies. "Oh, yes," she managed to murmur.

Josh looked at her attentively, as if trying to elicit another word from her mouth. Still, the words seemed trapped in her throat.

"If it's something I can do, I will," he said. "But my time is pretty limited."

As is mine, Hallie thought abruptly, almost looking at her watch. Her mind whirled in search of words. How could she just blurt out her need for a home room mother? Home room person, she corrected her thoughts. Leading up to the vital question might take time—time which she didn't have tonight.

She felt the pressure of a deep breath building. Just ask him and get it over with, she told herself. But getting a room person was important, she told herself. Getting the right one was even more important. She glanced at Josh quickly. When had she decided he was the *right* one?

She took a breath. "Nate's class needs a homeroom dad, a volunteer who helps out occasionally, like on field trips and classroom parties."

Josh didn't answer, and Hallie wondered if he was trying to think of a way to refuse nicely. "You'd want to accompany Nate on field trips anyway." She heard the uneasiness in her voice, and one hand reached to grasp the door handle, as if the metal support could shore up her fading confidence.

Her finger landed on the back of Josh's hand, and a spark, as fleeting as a wisp of summer lightning, touched her. It took a moment to move her hand casually and brush at a strand of hair, giving herself time to compose her thoughts. "You'd want to be present to inspect the cookies and cupcakes other parents bring to the classroom for the children's parties."

"You know what could happen. If Nate gets sick, I have to leave you in the lurch."

She looked up. The flare from the overhead light touched his eyes, reflecting a glow that made her think of candlelight and hearths. Her breath caught. Suddenly, it seemed very important that he didn't turn her request down.

"Maybe we could have a backup room mother."

Josh lifted his right hand, using one finger to sweep an errant strand of hair from her forehead. "It's an idea," Josh said, his voice husky.

"You'll think about it." Her gaze was mesmerized by the intent look of his darkening pupils.

He nodded slowly.

"I'll settle for a maybe." Her voice sounded throaty in her ears, and she felt vaguely disoriented. Were his lips only inches from hers? Had she leaned involuntarily toward him, willing him to close the distance between them?

In the background Hallie heard the tinkle of the store bell and then the sound of Nate's voice pealed across the parking lot.

"Miss Ember, Miss Ember, don't go. I'm awake."

Chapter Four

Sleepily Hallie turned off the alarm and swung her bare feet to the pine floor. Fishing! She'd actually accepted an invitation to go fishing this morning. She let out a noisy breath. She was a city girl. To her, fish were creatures who danced in tuna commercials before jumping gleefully into luxurious oil baths. She didn't know anything about fishing.

But how could she turn down the plea of the lovable youngster? The anticipation of meeting her writing friends in Hollywood had waned when she saw the invitation echo in the glow of Josh's eyes. Never mind that his voiced invitation had been less than enthusiastic.

She slid off the bed and padded down the hall to the bathroom. Twenty minutes later, clad in jeans and a hand-printed T-shirt lauding the beauty of San Diego, she walked softly down the stairs. Lydia's bedroom was on the lower level, and she wanted to avoid waking her boss.

The aroma of coffee met her, and she silently thanked Lydia for putting the coffee on the automatic timer. She found a mug and filled it with coffee. Glancing at her watch, she walked to open the sliding glass door leading to the patio and stepped outside. She breathed in the crisp air, her gaze roaming over the late-blooming blossoms in Lydia's backyard. The splash of brightness escalated the indescribably pleasant feeling that had started last evening.

She squinted through the pines at the sky and wondered if this was good fishing weather—not that she meant to bait a hook. She would drop a line into the water and occasionally ask why the fish were avoiding her hook. She was doing this for Nate, she told herself, and realized it was true. Almost. Not ready to let her thoughts question her actions, she watched an inquisitive gray squirrel who'd paused to turn alert, olive-black eyes in Hallie's direction. Satisfied that she was not hostile, he tilted his small, gray nose into the crisp morning air, turned his head one way and then the other, like a child waiting to cross a street, then scurried across the pine-needled ground in search of breakfast.

Hallie's thoughts returned involuntarily to the previous evening. Of course, she'd had to go back inside the store to coax the excited, dancing Nate out of the cool evening air. Somehow, time slipped away over hot chocolate and good conversation with the three attentive males. Nate had fallen asleep on the couch again by eight-thirty, but she hadn't left until after ten.

She turned at the sound of Lydia's voice.

"I thought you were going to the city last evening." The older woman stood in the doorway dressed in a colorful caftan that rivaled the flowers outside.

Hallie grinned. "I got delayed."

Lydia held up a plastic-wrapped pack. "You want one of these toaster things?"

Hallie eyed the tart, nodded, and followed Lydia inside.

"Probably better that you drive down in the daytime anyway. These winding roads take a little practice."

"I'm not going to the city."

Lydia opened the package, set the toaster, and lifted an eyebrow. "Not going? You were so eager to see your writing group."

"I know." Placing her cup on the island counter, Hallie slid onto a high stool. She tried to look regretful, but that indescribable feeling she attributed to the flowers and the mountain air still clung to her. "I'll go next week," she said lamely.

Lydia's brow creased. "Will your friend be worried when you don't show up?"

Worried, no. Irritated, yes. Candace believed that "being where the action is" was important. "I called her."

Lydia placed the heated tarts on plates and slid one across to Hallie. "I'm sorry if the meeting delayed you. I know this job is only temporary and your writing is important to you."

"It wasn't the meeting, Lydia." Hallie busied her eyes and fingers with the tart. "I stopped to see one of my students who'd been absent."

The older teacher took an experimental sip of coffee. "The Snow child," she said, as if she had a sixth sense.

Hallie nodded.

"Is he all right?"

"Seems to be. Nate's father thought Nate might be catching a cold." The memory of Josh's loving look at his son flashed by. No doubt, he gave his wife the same look, she mused, and wondered why that thought arose.

"So why aren't you going to L.A. this morning?"

"Nate asked me to go fishing." She met Lydia's interested look with a lame grin.

A sparkle touched Lydia's eyes. "Is Nathan's father planning to accompany you?"

Hallie stared at Lydia, laughter building at the thought of trying to manage a five-year-old and a fishing pole in the same morning. She giggled. "I hope so. I scarcely know which end of the hook the worm rides on, let alone which way to turn that reel thing."

Lydia smiled. "It'll be good for you. You might get to like the mountains and apply for a full-time job."

Hallie rolled her eyes.

"It's just a thought. Good teachers are hard to find."

Hallie blinked, feeling the pleasure and acceptance the words brought. "Thank you."

Lydia nodded, lifting the coffee pot toward Hallie.

"No. I'd better go." Hallie rose and moved to place her cup in the dishwasher.

"You'll need a light jacket and a hat. The sun gets pretty bright on the water, and a breeze may come up later."

Hallie blinked. Where was her head this morning? She should have remembered a jacket. She ran up the stairs to her room. Picking up a sheaf of papers that had fallen from the printer, she placed them on her makeshift desk and hurried to the closet. She'd worked on the new script for two hours to soothe her nagging conscience.

Finding a light jacket, she pulled it over the T-shirt and went back down the stairs. Lydia waited with a straw hat. "Have a good day," she added.

Driving faster than usual, Hallie pressed the brake, admonishing herself to take the next curve slower. She wasn't *that* eager to go fishing, she told herself wryly. True, she continued to converse with herself, she felt something special for Nate. And Josh's look of admiration went a long way in assuaging the humiliation of being dumped by the actor. She'd returned Josh's teasing, telling herself the friendly repartee was just that. Any relationship was as insubstantial as the occasional rainbow over the lake. Her stay in the mountains was temporary. She rounded another curve. Better yet, the urge to disavow any attraction to Josh was mute. The way he pulled back at times showed he was still in love with the memory of his wife.

Nate had a kindergartner's crush on her, of course. Maybe Josh's feeling were similar. A crush on Josh's teacher in gratitude for her concern for his son. No doubt her imagination, spurred by the murmuring pines and lapping water and the electrifying spark she felt when she touched Josh's hand, let her read more into his look than he'd intended.

If she was absolutely clinical about the scene last evening, one might say Josh had been nothing more than a father being kind to his son's teacher. She'd wanted more because she needed to feel she was attractive to someone.

Parking at the side of the country store, she closed the car door firmly, as if she'd settled an argument. She'd be on her way back to the city in a few months. She'd dated other men before the actor—why wouldn't she now? Today, Josh Snow's beguiling grin and attentiveness would be viewed for just what they were: courteous attention because she was his son's teacher.

Josh placed the bowl of microwaved oatmeal on the table beside the orange juice and prepared for Nate's "Ah, Dad" look of exasperation. The predictable lift of the five-year-old's eyelids was on time. Josh was prepared. He straightened his shoulders imperceptibly, controlled his mouth so his lips wouldn't give him away, and returned his son's look with the usual we're-not-taking-one-step-out-of-the-store-until-you-finish-eating stare.

His lips almost quivered when Nate breathed out noisily, letting him know it took a great deal of patience to cope with a backward parent who didn't watch television commercials. Josh repressed his sigh. Practicing parenting in competition with sugary breakfasts-to-go commercials wasn't easy. Tough love started early.

Josh scooped the drinks and snacks he'd assembled earlier in one hand, draped two jackets over the same arm, and started for the stairs. One hand on the rail, he paused, looking back. Nate shoveled cereal into his mouth methodically, and Josh winced. What would it hurt to forgo breakfast one morning?

"It takes a bunch of energy to reel in a fish," he said cheerfully. "See ya downstairs." He breathed out heavily. It was hard to deny Nate anything, even going fishing without breakfast. But parents had to be responsible, and he, more than some others.

He'd been up hours before Nate. He'd checked the tackle box, packed snacks and beverages, and found a rod and reel for Hallie. Still, he had time to think of Nate's teacher, thoughts he'd tried to dismiss. There was no need to wish for a life he couldn't have. He had Nate. Someday, he might think about a single woman with children, someone who didn't want to bear more children.

He put the jackets beside the fishing gear in the rec room. Maybe asking Hallie on the fishing trip was a mistake. But Nate had been so eager. How could he deny his son the pleasure of his teacher's company? Not to mention the pleasure it would bring his son's father, even if he knew her nearness now would bring him pain later.

At the sound of the bell, Josh pushed aside the plastic panels in the store. Hallie stood in the doorway, sunlight bouncing off her hair to form a misty tiara. The thudding in his chest seemed like a drum heralding the arrival of a princess. He blinked, realizing his son's eagerness had little to do with the feeling of anticipation that had been building in *his* chest.

Twenty minutes later, a reel in one hand, a Thermos in the other, Hallie relinquished the reel to let Josh help her into a small boat. Nate followed, plopped onto a cushioned bench, and reached for a life jacket. Turning back to Josh, Hallie extended her arms to accept the array of equipment he thrust toward her.

"I didn't know it took so much stuff to catch a little fish," Hallie said cheerfully. She lowered a plastic box and reached for another bag.

"Food for the humans as well as the fish," Josh replied. He grinned and Hallie saw his face was already relaxing, the lines around his mouth softening. He moved to release the rope holding the boat to the dock before he jumped lithely into the boat.

"All aboard," he shouted cheerfully.

"We're going out to see the sea," Nathan chimed in.

Josh grinned self-consciously at Hallie. "Our little joke." He bent to distribute the cooler, tackle box, fishing gear, and Thermos throughout the boat to his satisfaction, then looked at Nate, peering at the straps of the life jacket before he moved to start the motor. The motor coughed and grumbled awake like a grouchy bear protesting the end of his hibernation. Hallie glanced at Nate, but he paid little attention to the motor. Checking his fishing reel took a lot of concentration.

Feeling a tap on her arm, Hallie looked aside. Josh's lips moved, but the motor covered his words. She leaned closer, catching the scent of soap special to Josh, and gazed down as his fingers pointed to the cushion on her seat.

"The cushion also serves as a float." He mouthed the words, touched the cushion beside him, and indicated the straps on each side by slipping a hand through one belt.

Hallie nodded and Josh backed the boat slowly away from the dock. He paused to peer at Nate's life jacket again. Apparently assured the straps were secure, he turned the boat and they moved slowly across the sun-dappled water.

Hallie sat tensely on the cushioned seat as the boat skimmed over the surface of the gray-blue water. A few small boats cruised the waterway slowly; others parked on the water while their drivers cast lines beneath the glittering surface. Then the boat slowed and the motor softened to a gruff purr before it became silent. She glanced at Josh. His broad shoulders stretched the fabric of his cotton shirt as he reached over the steering wheel to retrieve a pair of sunglasses and a billed cap. Sunlight gilded his hair and bathed his cheeks with a healthy glow, and Hallie felt a tremor beneath her ribcage. She'd thought of him as a wonderful father and a kind, caring person. She hadn't thought of him as handsome until she looked at his beautifully shaped head, his firm jawline, and generous lips. He pulled the billed cap on and turned toward her, and she shifted her gaze quickly before he could catch her observing him.

A short distance away, two boats bobbed silently on the water. She cleared her throat, as if breaking the silence between them would erase the tremor toying with the tips of her nerves.

"I assume this is the fishing spot."

"Were you hoping we wouldn't find one?" Amusement flickered in his eyes before he raised his sunglasses, fitting the curved wires over his ears.

"Am I so transparent?" She hoped her sunglasses concealed any sign of the effect his velvety voice had on her already wobbly nerves. She hadn't reckoned on the size of the boat making their nearness a necessity and reactivating earlier feelings.

Somehow she'd thought the young fisherman on the bench and occupants of nearby boats would keep any anxiety over their togetherness at a minimum. This was supposed to be a fishing trip for Nate, a casual, relaxing outing. But her body wasn't cooperating.

Josh moved to the bench in the middle of the boat, opening the tackle box to remove a small jar filled with miniature red balls. "We don't use worms."

Hallie breathed an exaggerated sigh. "You could have told me earlier and saved me all this stress."

"Don't you like worms, Miss Ember?" Nate's eyes widened in consternation. "They're nice."

Hallie smiled bravely. "I like worms. Just not on fishhooks."

Nate's eagerness to get his hook into the water took precedence over his concern with wriggly creatures. He extended his rod toward his father, watching studiously as Josh tied a barb to the end of the line and covered it with the red stuff from the jar.

When Josh tied a hook to her line, Hallie reached for the jar, as if to bait her own hook, and waited for Josh to turn his attention to Nate before she lowered an unbaited barb into the water.

They "fished" in relative silence, except for an occasional query from Josh asking his son if he'd had any nibbles. Once he had Nate reel in the line and added more bait to a bare barb. He remained on the bench within reaching distance of Nate, but his protectiveness wasn't evident to the boy.

Though the darkened lenses of his glasses hid his eyes, Hallie had felt his gaze on her more than once. But he'd only shown her polite friendliness—the attention he'd show any guest before he retreated into silence.

Was he thinking of his wife? Wishing she was the one sitting in the closely confined quarters of the small boat with him and his son? It was only natural, Hallie told herself. It would be difficult to let her memory go, this woman who must have been a paragon of motherhood to withstand the stress of constant vigilance and midnight hospital runs.

Was she a fourth person in the boat on this serene lake with the sun shaking bits of glitter over the water? Did Josh miss her so much he couldn't mention her name? Had he found her so ideal no other woman could fill her shoes?

Hallie scolded herself. The thoughts weren't appropriate. She was a temporary teacher in a mountain school, and she meant to return to the city as soon as possible. From what Josh said, Nate's health didn't thrive in the smog-laden air of populous urban areas.

The sound of Josh's voice interrupted her thoughts.

"Looks like someone caught something."

She followed Josh's gaze across the bright water to an exuberant fisherman, the tip of his pole raised to allow his companion to net a dancing fish.

She glanced at Nate, prepared to encourage him, but before she could speak, Josh's voice echoed her thoughts.

"Hey, Nate, I'll bet the fish are in line to take your bait. They just can't agree on who goes first." Josh paused. "Maybe fresh bait will help them make up their minds," he said in a positive note.

A smile quivered on Hallie's lips. Odd how their thoughts had coincided. Nate flicked his gaze toward his father and turned the handle on his reel with dubious enthusiasm, and she wondered if Josh felt a pebble in his throat as she did. Without glancing at his rod, she realized he hadn't had a nibble, as far as she could tell. The smile quivered again. Had Josh, too, left his hook bare to let Nate catch the first fish?

Half an hour later, Nate's gasp alerted the other occupants of the boat to a change of events.

"Dad." The word was breathless, triumphant, and an unrestrained plea for help.

Hallie looked at both males in turn. Nate clenched one youthful hand on the amber fiberglass rod and struggled to turn the handle on the reel.

Hallie didn't need to see behind the darkened lenses of Josh's glasses. His delight radiated in his mouth, cheeks, and body movements. "I told you they were waitin' in line, dude." He grinned at Hallie, assuring himself she shared the joy of this momentous event, before he turned his attention back to his son and the wobbling rod in his youthful hands.

Under Josh's quiet guidance, the fish appeared, its colorful scales shimmering as it tail-danced on the water. Josh reached for the line, pulling the shimmying dancer near and gently removed the hook. "How'd you do that, Nate? I haven't had one nibble all morning."

Nate's face was radiant.

Josh turned to Hallie, displaying the dancer, allowing her to marvel at his son's ability.

"Nate, it's your turn to teach me something about fishing." Involuntarily, her voice rose in animation, sparking a self-conscious grin on Nate's face and a ricochet in her chest at Josh's beam of approval.

Josh removed his glasses to peer studiously at the trout before turning to his son. His exaggerated sigh was accompanied by a slow shake of his head and a look as sorrowful as a hound dog who'd failed to tree his prey.

"I'm afraid this one needs to go back in the water and grow a little, Nate. He's not big enough to keep."

Brief disappointment pursed Nate's mouth. Then he nodded with stoic resignation, not at all upset as far as Hallie could tell, and watched his father lean forward to release the colorful fish. Hallie breathed easier as the shimmying dancer slid beneath the surface of the water. She doubted fishing could ever become her favorite hobby.

Nate's disappointment erupted later, when at the end of another hour Josh suggested Nate pull up his fishing line.

"Aw, Dad. Just a little longer."

"If I'm going to make blueberry pancakes before I start to work in the store, we need to pack it in. We don't want Paul working too long and getting tired, do we?"

"I guess not," Nate grumbled. He turned the handle of the reel reluctantly.

"You will join us, won't you?" Josh's voice hovered in the polite host mode.

Nate's exuberant voice made up for it. "Dad makes great bruberry pancakes. I put on the whipped cream."

Hallie busied her fingers reeling in her fishing line. She should leave now. She'd gone fishing with Nate. She could still drive into the city. Still see her friends. Still chase her goal. She'd done more than was expected of a teacher. Nate was appealing, and Josh was attractive, but she'd be moving in a few months.

Josh removed his glasses and grinned at his son. Then he looked at Hallie. "You will, won't you?" he repeated. His voice warmed, and the look in his eyes echoed the hopeful invitation of his son. "Join us for breakfast? My pancakes are still in the novice-chef stage, but think of the company." He grinned in self-deprecation.

Hallie pulled the line in and with meticulous care, secured the fishhook. Even that didn't allow her time to control her thoughts. Refusing Nate's bubbling invitation was ludicrous. She had to eat sometime.

With the boat tied to the dock again, Hallie lifted her share of the fishing gear and joined her impatient young host. While Josh walked behind them, Nate talked nonstop about the fish and the blueberry pancakes. He paused briefly to glance at a small gray squirrel who darted across the path. When Josh held the door of the market open, Nate rushed inside, bypassing two browsing customers.

"Paul, I caught a big one," he chortled breathlessly. "But Dad said we should put it back so it could grow."

"Good idea," Paul agreed cheerfully. He looked at Josh. "Want me to stay a while longer?"

Josh walked behind the counter. "Would you? I thought I'd fix breakfast and lunch at the same time."

"You got me," Paul replied. He looked at Nate. "You want to stay and tell me about the fishing?"

Nate wrinkled his brow in indecision. "I'd better help Dad. He's going to make bruberry pancakes."

Paul nodded solemnly. "You can tell me another time."

"I'll show you the way, Miss Ember," Nate said.

Holding the plastic slats aside, Josh waved toward a corner of the rec room. "You can put your rod in the corner."

Upstairs, he directed her to the bathroom to wash

up. When she rejoined him, Nate was rewashing his hands under his father's stern eye.

"What can I do?" Hallie asked.

"Plates in the cupboard on your right. Silverware in the drawer below." He laughed. "This is an important occasion, having someone to breakfast. We use paper plates when Nate and I eat. Saves dishwashing time."

Setting the table by the window, Hallie paused to admire the view. In the distance, the brilliant colors of a parasail lifted over the sun-bathed water. Near the shore, three children kicked water at each other while an adult held an unread book in her hand.

"What a wonderful place to live," Hallie said. "Besides having a marvelous view, you don't have to fight freeway traffic to go to work."

Josh poured pancake mix into a bowl. "That's not always a perk." He chuckled. "You really can't get away from your work when it's down one flight of stairs."

Hallie lifted an eyebrow.

"If someone wants a loaf of bread at three in the morning, they knock on the door and explain they're going fishing at five and have to fix sandwiches. As if that explains the whole thing." He grinned. "But we had people waking us up at three in the morning in Los Angeles. So I guess there's little difference. And as you said, I'm not fighting the freeway traffic."

"What did someone wake you up for at three in the morning in L.A.?"

"My partner and I had a computer business. We

promised help at any time. Some of our customers were losing business if their computers were down."

"So you decided you might as well enjoy the scenery if you had to get up at three?"

"It was more a matter of survival, Nate's and mine. Mainly, the air in the mountains is better for Nate. The decreased stress is better for me."

"Stress?"

"Every nanny I hired for Josh called so often about his health, I finally decided I needed a job where I could keep an eye on him myself. A small market sounded just right."

Pushing the bowl aside, Josh stepped to the refrigerator to remove a package of blueberries. He reached back inside for a package of bacon. "Do you want to put bacon slices between paper towels?" He looked at Hallie. "Easier for me to cook bacon in the microwave."

Hallie nodded, moving to the counter near him. He hadn't mentioned Nate's mother. Hallie wondered when she had died.

Blueberry pancakes were no problem, Josh conceded, if one had a microwave and a market with a frozen food section. But with a guest, he thought making them looked better. He'd brought the mix and frozen blueberries upstairs last evening, hoping Hallie would accept their invitation.

He looked up briefly, seeing Hallie put aside the bacon and move to the plate-glass window in response to a call from Nate. He took a deep breath. The kitchen seemed warmer than usual, and he hadn't even turned on a stove burner yet. Of course, he had been rushing to get breakfast started. But he was usually in a hurry: a hurry to get Nate to school, a hurry to get Nate home from school, a hurry to fix him something to eat before the bell in the store sounded. So why was the kitchen warmer today?

He placed the griddle on the stove, turned on a burner, and moved his bowl near. The obvious answer stood a few feet away, engrossed in Nate's animated explanation about the patrol boat on the lake. Josh lowered his gaze to the griddle, testing the surface with a drop of water. The water danced on the heated iron, dribbling away slowly. But his musing didn't.

Hallie wasn't exactly unaware of the attraction between them, and she seemed fond of Nate. He reined in his thoughts. No matter how attractive the school-teacher looked or how much she liked Nate or how many signals she sent, he couldn't respond in kind. He had all the problems he could handle, past, present, and future. None of them would improve by his becoming involved with this sexy lady. Not that he had to worry about a future with the teacher. Once he divulged his problem, she'd be just like his ex-wife.

He'd be the one that was hurt. He wasn't willing to cope with that again. He and Nate were doing all right. Nate would be happier with a family, complete with mother, siblings, and maybe resident grandparents. But for now, Nate had a father who tried to be all things to him.

He tested the grill again, watching the water sizzle

and disappear. He stirred the batter. The one way Nate might have a family is if his father could find a compatible lady willing to share children and grandparents.

Even that was iffy. Sibyl's exasperated words echoed in his mind. "Nate's too much to cope with. I don't think I could handle it even if he was. . . ." He could still see the anguish in her eyes at the slip in speech.

He should have known then, but he was still in a stage that cherished the notion she loved him enough to abide any human frailty. He'd been wrong.

Being a responsible, faithful, and loving husband who'd cared for her and Nate, as his father had taken care of his family, hadn't been enough.

Could he expect the lovely Hallie would not be the same? One couldn't blame any woman for wanting what Sibyl had wanted.

He poured a dollop of batter on the heated griddle. Perhaps he should look for a family for Nate. It might keep his mind off the lovely teacher. He'd noticed the young woman with three children the first day of school. When he'd heard she was a widow, he'd wryly thought she'd make an ideal choice. But he hadn't really considered her a candidate for the role of Nate's mother. He dropped another dollop of batter on the iron. Maybe he should. Maybe romancing the widow would keep thoughts of Hallie at bay.

He could invite the widow's son, Robby, to visit Nate. The mother would need to pick him up. It was a beginning, a way to keep his mind off the kindergarten teacher. He mustn't keep thinking of Hallie. He couldn't let the lovely lady arouse feelings that hadn't a snowflake's chance to survive on a sizzling griddle.

He knew he should tell her he couldn't volunteer for the homeroom dad thing. Even on an occasional basis, working with her upset his equilibrium.

He scooped the warm pancakes onto a platter. "Hey, you two. Breakfast is ready."

Seated across from Hallie, he watched her search beneath the mound of cream peaked on her pancakes. Nate had been generous with the spray can.

"Mmmm," she murmured in appreciation.

"I told you you'd like my dad's bruberry pancakes." Nate decorated the snowy mountain on his plate with a berry peak.

"You were right." Hallie touched the tip of her tongue to a smudge of cream on her lip. "I'm glad I listened to you."

Josh glanced fondly at the two people across from him. A strange feeling rose in his throat, but his voice was light when he spoke. "I'd like to say I'm sorry you missed your trip to the city, Hallie, but I'd be fibbing. It's nice to have company."

"It's nice to *be* company," Hallie returned. "I'll go to the city next weekend. I doubt that my friend will move before then."

Josh's breath idled like a cold motor. He wondered if she had a male friend she'd planned to see, and he realized he didn't like the thought.

"I'll call her this evening and catch up on the industry news."

Josh breathed more easily. "Industry news?" A dollop of cream stuck to his upper lip.

Nate giggled. "Daddy, you got a mustache."

Josh shaved the mustache with his napkin and looked toward Hallie expectantly.

"I'm a screenwriter." She laughed self-consciously. "I haven't sold a script, but I've written a lot. Industry news to me is who's buying what and who's looking for what kind of story. I get together with other writers, and we talk and eat and console each other."

Josh nodded, a strange feeling bubbling inside him like warm lava, and took another bite of pancake. His cooking was pretty good. Nate had caught a fish. The sun was shining. And Miss Hallie Ember wasn't going to the city to see a "him."

Chapter Five

Hallie's Thursday afternoon classroom was in what she had begun to think of as normal—controlled chaos.

Patiently, she moved to forestall a kindergartner's efforts to shove his arms through a tangle of straps. "You don't need your backpack, Robby." She returned the pack to a carton. Watching the youngster scamper to join his classmates, Hallie warily scanned the classroom for novice travelers who'd misunderstood her directions.

Neither the student's eager scramble to form a reasonably straight line or the awareness that Josh would accompany her on the trip did a lot to suspend Hallie's anxiety. She counted heads again and sighed: one less than at her last count.

Locating the dawdling youngster in the restroom, she returned to find the line scrambled. She took a calming breath. It was natural for the children to think she could find the missing student faster with a little help.

Urging the dawdler forward, she watched in amazement as the students realigned into a column. The promise of a ride on the school's minibus seemed to work wonders. She sent a message to her lips to curve upward, hoping the signal would loosen her lungs as well as her looks. For goodness sakes! She'd survived the opening day of school. Even more challenging, she'd survived the wait for an answer to the first script she'd sent to an agent. How difficult could a field trip be?

It was only a shopping tour to the local greeting card shop. The parents had been informed, and the majority had sent in the prerequisite cost of a card. Josh wasn't the only parent accompanying the children, and the other two mothers looked alert and responsible. And Anna had returned.

Surely, they couldn't lose a child between the minibus and the entrance to the store. The mountain city was not Los Angeles. Nevertheless, her wavering smile sagged. She'd carefully instructed the children on the ground rules. She'd talked to the shop owner. She'd enlisted adequate adult supervision. What could go wrong?

She trailed the excited students, her own adrenaline barely under control, and stepped outside. Beyond the schoolyard, towering pines filtered the midday sun, but in the parking lot, sunlight bouncing off the school bus blinded Hallie momentarily. She moved away from the glare and saw Josh standing near the bus. For some inexplicable reason, his presence soothed the trepidation plaguing her. She smiled confidently, counted heads again, factoring in the two absentees, and made a thumbs-up sign to Anna.

With the children and adults on the bus, she found her place on the front seat. The minibus motor purred, and she leaned back and breathed. They were underway.

Somewhere, amid worrying about losing a child in the shop, she thought about the call to Candace last evening. It was her third call to her writing friend about a plot problem with the limo-driver-and-attorney story. They'd talked about the success of a mutual friend and the returned script of another. Then the bus slowed, and she was a teacher again.

Inside the store, she paused, allowing the other adults to access their surroundings and direct their groups in the right direction. The shop was small and cozy, with assorted gifts on shelves and tables, and in glass cases.

Awed, the somewhat subdued students shuffled toward plastic cases displaying an array of colorful artwork. They were under the wary gaze of the supervisors, but Hallie told herself not to relax yet. Aware Josh was nearby, she stopped by the students led by Robby's mother, Marianne. Nate and Robby peered at the cards studiously.

Hallie bent forward. "Who are you sending a card to?"

Nate didn't look up. "Grandpa and Grandma. They live a long way from here." His gaze lingered on a colorful design of clowns and balloons. "Do you think they'd like this one?"

Hallie took the card from the showcase and read the message inside to Nate. Then she handed it to him, waiting for him to study the card. Finally, he looked up. "Is that the one you want?"

Nate nodded. "Grandpa will like the clown. He said he'd take me to the circus when he comes to see us."

Hallie spoke to Marianne and showed Nate the way to the checkout counter. She stepped aside, allowing Nate to hand his money to the cheerful clerk. The clerk counted out the change to Nate, then placed the card in a purple plastic bag and handed it to Nate. Hallie looked up to see Josh watching the transaction, and his gaze lifted to hers. A feeling of warmth surrounded her, and she smiled, sharing her pride in Nate's accomplishment with his father.

She waited for Robby to purchase his card and ushered the pair back to their group.

"Robby is sleeping over Friday night," Nate informed her.

"That's nice," Hallie said warmly. Josh was amazing. As if he didn't have enough to do, what with working in the store and worrying over his son, he could still find time to invite someone to visit Nate.

The object of her thoughts moved into view, urging the students toward the bus. With their earlier eagerness waning, the shoppers started to reboard the bus. Hallie felt her pulse quicken as Josh stopped beside her.

"It's going well, so far," he said cheerfully.

His look held the warmth of subdued laughter she'd noticed when their gaze locked over pride in Nathan's card purchase. Then he moved away with the students.

His words and look still lingered, filling her with a pleasant feeling. They agreed in so many ways— maybe too many! Or was she seeing something that wasn't there? Was she looking for someone to deny the actor's assessment of her character? His words had hurt. Was she looking for confirmation that he'd been wrong? That she wasn't so wrapped up in her paper people that she couldn't empathize with real people? Even fall in love? The thought troubled her. Even more troubling was the thought that she might, un-wittingly, be using Josh as a test. She shook her head mentally. She cared for Nate and Josh. She refused to think how much. She'd been writing so long, waiting so long to sell a script. She couldn't succeed if she didn't remember that writing came first.

She looked toward the bus where Josh and Anna were guiding the students aboard and saw Josh turn to speak to Robby's mother, no doubt confirming their plans for the boys' weekend. She pushed aside a sud-den feeling of loneliness at the sound of their laughter. She had plans of her own this weekend.

At the school, Hallie watched Josh drive from the parking lot with mixed feelings. The bus had returned without losing one student, and the parents had picked up their children. Despite a noticeable concern that Nate might be overtired, Josh had lingered, as if to assure himself that Hallie's first field trip had gone well. "Kindergarten Dad" had even inquired as to the next appearance she had scheduled for him. She didn't know when the next event was planned but she intended to make it as soon as possible.

On Friday afternoon, Hallie left the mountains with a muted feeling of accomplishment. She was on her way to the city, so why wasn't she elated?

She drove past the turnoff to the mountain store and tried to think about the coming weekend. Instead, she wondered if Josh had invited Robby's mother to go fishing with him and the boys.

Josh kept interrupting her thoughts even when she reached the city. Amid her circle of writing friends, she found herself thinking of the paternal fondness in Josh's eyes over Nate's excitement when he'd caught a fish. And the way he'd grinned at her, as if they shared a secret. She was even a little irritated when she heard her name and realized she should be listening to the latest gossip at the script mill.

Later, accompanying her friend Candace to a party, she'd been thrilled when a well-known producer asked her to dance. But she barely listened to his comments on current trends in screenwriting as she wondered if Josh would cook pancakes for Robby and his mother. Dancing with a fledgling actor, who could have given Brad Pitt competition in the looks department, she found herself wishing that the arms that held her belonged to the market owner.

She'd admonished herself to get real. The fisherman/father/storekeeper lived in the mountains, and she would be returning to the city shortly.

She gave the actor her roommate's phone number, had dinner with him on Saturday, and promised to call him when she returned to the city. On Sunday, she reminded herself that tomorrow was a school day, and Robby Lewis and another student had birthdays this week. She needed to alert the kindergarten room father to the expected celebrations. Involuntary feelings stirred in her, roaming in reckless abandonment of the obstacles to anything but a casual relationship with Nate's father.

She drove back to the mountains earlier than she'd planned.

Sunday evening, she called Josh to apprise him of the upcoming birthdays. "Their mothers will bring cookies or cupcakes. I'll have to ask about punch."

"I can do punch," Josh said.

Hallie replaced the receiver dreamily and strolled to her computer. She was in just the mood to get Cindy Ellen, the limo driver, and the reluctant attorney together.

Guiding the irregular line of Friday afternoon students toward the schoolyard, Hallie scanned the area for Josh. He'd left Nate, saying he'd return to set up for the party during the recess period. She followed the children into the yard, moving to scan the parking lot. Calm down, she coaxed her nerves. It's not like you're going to a party for a Hollywood heavyweight. Just kindergarten kids, kindergarten parents—that's all. One of them might be a little special, but he's a dad . . . a *dad*, she emphasized, not a television or movie producer.

Josh arrived minutes after the pint-sized students had returned to the classroom. Expecting him didn't deter the catch in Hallie's breath when the door opened, nor the swell in her chest when he appeared in the doorway. Juggling cartons of punch, Josh paused, holding the door open with one brawny shoulder for someone to enter. Marianne Lewis brushed past him, a covered basket in one hand and a floating bouquet of colorful inflated hearts and assorted balloons in the other. For a fleeting moment, Hallie wondered if they had come together. The airy swell in her chest threatened to deflate, as if pricked by a pin. Then Josh closed the door, smiled, and lifted his shoulders in apology for his tardiness. The pinprick closed, allowing the airy feeling to soar again.

Reluctantly, Hallie assumed her teacher's hat, though her attention was as distracted as that of her students. Her gaze kept straying to the volunteers.

When the door opened again, she noted a new arrival and Josh's conversation with the man, who had delivered a covered tray.

Leaving Anna with the children, she went to thank the parent for his contribution, hearing enough of the conversation to realize that Josh was checking on the ingredients of the refreshments.

Cory's father, she noted, filing his identity in her mind as he left. She turned to Josh. "Everything going okay?"

Josh nodded. "Cory's father delivered the cookies

his wife baked before she left for work. Chocolate chip, raisin, and sugar cookies." He lowered the plastic tray to the table, his look at Hallie warm and relaxed. "Nate has no problem with chocolate, walnuts, raisins, and sugar." He swept a hand toward Marianne's display of paper plates and napkins. "Look all right?" He followed Hallie's gaze. "Paper cups," he said. "I forgot to bring in the paper cups for the punch."

Twenty minutes later, Hallie surmised that the party was a success, especially if the noise level counted as a rating gauge. Colorful balloons dipped and swayed over the refreshment table. Paper chains with birthday messages—a class contribution—trailed haphazardly between chairs and tables, and every youthful body was in perpetual motion.

One adventurous partygoer snagged the end of a paper chain and ran haphazardly around the room to ensnare his classmates. Swerving dangerously close to the refreshment table, he giggled when he bumped the table. Swiftly, Josh moved to catch the wobbling punch bowl and became entangled in the chain. Steadying the bowl, he tried to release his hips from the chain without breaking the paper.

Hallie weaved through the mob of youngsters. "Regretting your volunteer job?" Hallie teased.

"No more than you seem to regret your substitute job." He pushed the paper downward and stepped over the chain. Soft laughter erupted as their looks met.

He's enjoying this, Hallie thought, and realized that she was also. The children were so natural and uninhibited—far more fun than the adults at the party she'd attended last weekend.

Which reminded her, she hadn't packed for her trip to the city this weekend, which was special. She was going to have lunch with her agent.

"Can I get you a cup of punch?" Josh asked. "My own blend."

Hallie looked at the large plastic bowl filled with a rosy liquid. "Orange slices and what? Those red things I see in the punch? They look like cherries."

"You're right, cherries. I added a couple of jars of candied cherries and a little soda to make it more interesting."

"You make a good homeroom father." She accepted the punch, taking a sip without moving her look from his. "Mmm, you make a good punch too."

"Thank you, ma'am." Josh dipped his head, his face serious, but his eyes twinkling.

A soft body thudded against Hallie's hip and she looked down to see a ponytailed child pushing an empty cup upward. "Looks like you have another customer." She moved away from the table. She glanced toward Marianne, then Anna, wondering if they'd noticed her with Josh at the punch bowl. Had she lingered too long? Had an involuntary rapt expression betrayed her? With a casualness she didn't feel, she moved to help a youngster carry cookies and a drink to the table.

Something was wrong. The noise level in the room hadn't abated. Joyful shrieks and laughter bubbled over the sound of thudding feet. But she felt like a mother hen whose antennae have been alerted to a break in the rhythm of her chicklets' voices. Her gaze scanned the room, over the laughing children, skirting Marianne at the punch bowl, to Anna replenishing the cookie plates, to Josh amid a group of children.

His expression was different—not the earlier humorous grin nor the past wariness she'd seen. His expression was changing from cautious to downright anxiety as he weaved his way purposefully through the hip-high horde. He moved quickly, avoiding tiny toes and ill-balanced plates. Hallie's gaze scanned the children rapidly, searching for Nate, knowing immediately the source of Josh's concern. Panic sucked the air from her lungs. Josh reached Nate before her gaze found him. The kindergartner's head dipped forward, his tousled fair hair obscuring his eyes as he struggled to draw in air.

By the time Hallie reached his side, Josh was holding a chocolate chip cookie, disintegrating it in the crush of his fingers.

"Peanuts!" His voice ripped through the air, the crushed contents of his hand dropping on the floor as he scooped his son into his arms. "Who puts peanuts in chocolate chip cookies?"

His car was roaring out of the parking lot before Hallie took half a dozen steps out of the classroom.

Her eyes glazed as the speeding car disappeared. Behind her, shrieks and laughter rose and fell like waves in a boat's wake, and she knew she had to return to her charges. Switching her mind to remote control, she turned and reentered the room. She couldn't fall apart now, or go with Josh, no matter how much as she wanted to be with him.

She scanned the party scene, a part of her relieved to see that most of the revelers hadn't noticed the incident. Marianne was trying to keep an eye on the children while leaning over to comfort Robby. Seeing Hallie, she straightened, concern in her eyes. "Robby was standing next to Nate," she explained, almost apologizing for her son's tears. "But I don't think the other children realized what was happening."

Hallie looked at the milling students apprehensively. "Can you and Anna keep things going while I alert the office?"

Marianne nodded, and Hallie moved to apprise Anna of her errand.

She was grateful when her employer returned to the classroom with her, and even more grateful that the party was coming to a close. She glimpsed parents and sitters arriving to reclaim their charges. Panic trembling barely beneath her surface social civility, she ushered the last student through the door. The mother paused, giving her son a meaningful look.

Hallie gripped the doorknob fiercely. Any other time, she was definitely in favor of reminding children of good manners. She forced herself to breathe and let the young student utter a hesitant thank-you, and managed a smile at the shuffling reveler and his mother.

Doubting she could control her tattered nerves ten minutes longer, she left Marianne and Anna to close her room and hurried to her car.

She barely stayed below the speed limit driving to

the hospital that served the mountain community—
only to wait impatiently in the emergency unit waiting
room. Hurry up, and wait, she thought, restrained hys-
teria nibbling at her nerve endings again.

She'd identified herself, explained her concern to an
understanding nurse on duty, and been forgotten. Or
so she thought, until Josh spoke her name. He sat
down in the plastic-covered chair beside her with an
air of weariness.

Hallie looked at him anxiously, almost afraid to ask
about Nate's condition. As if he sensed her apprehen-
sion, he reached to let his fingers touch her hand gently.

"Nate's breathing easier," he said quietly.

Hallie closed her eyes, taking a deep breath slowly
a moment later. The tenseness, clutching her body like
a giant vise since she'd watched Josh race from the
classroom, ebbed slightly along with the expelled air.
She raised her eyelids and found Josh looking at her.

"Thank you for coming." His fingers hadn't moved
since he had placed them on her hand, but something
in his look made her acutely aware of them now. They
were as warm as the look in his eyes.

He blinked and pulled his gaze away, as he did his
fingers, and she wondered if he regretted the momentary closeness. When he spoke, his voice was dispas-
sionate.

"The nurse is moving him out of the emergency
room to the medical floor." He breathed deeply, as if
he, too, felt an easing of anxiety. "If I get Nate to the
hospital at the onset of an acute attack, the nurse starts

oxygen and a respiratory therapist begins the breathing treatments that relieve the swelling of his airways. Once the treatments and intravenous drugs ease the constriction, he starts to breathe easier."

"You sound like you know the routine." Hallie kept her voice light despite her continued concern.

Josh's fingers kneaded the plastic arm of the chair. "I've been through this more times than I care to remember."

Hallie peered at him compassionately, her fingers aching to reach forward and touch his tousled hair, to stroke his ashen face. Her right hand lifted imperceptibly before she lowered it, clasping her hands firmly together and resting them in her lap. She was seldom at a loss for words on paper, if editing her work was any measure. So why was her throat as clogged as a beaver dam when she wanted to say something reassuring and supportive? Moisture stung her eyes. Josh, she breathed his name silently. She understood his panic, knowing hers could not equal it. But she cared—deeply. She was beginning to realize how deeply.

Josh cleared his throat. "I feel a little more confident when the hospital and some of the personnel are familiar. Nate and I visited the doctor as soon as we moved to the mountains and then the emergency room. But the nursing roster changes, and the doctor is seldom the first one on the scene." His eyes were bleak. "It can be a nightmare when you try to tell some nurses what Nate needs." He sighed heavily. "I guess they see me as interfering. But I know Nate panics, and his breathing gets worse when the medical personnel rush me out of the room."

He lifted his drooping shoulders and eyed the door to the emergency room as if he was neglecting his post. "I know the medications Nate responds to. . . ." He paused and emitted strained laughter. "The worst is over when I start talking too much."

Hallie smiled weakly, another ounce of tension draining away at his words. "I'll try to remember that."

"Let's hope it's a long, long time before it's necessary." He made a wry face.

Nate's panicked look at his father as his breath whistled from his throat raked across Hallie's memory like a tiger's claw. She nodded solemnly. "Cory's mother learned about the cookie incident when she came to pick up her child. She told Marianne she had run out of walnuts and didn't have time to go to the store, so she'd substituted peanuts. She is terribly upset."

Josh nodded grimly. "Substituting peanuts made little difference to anyone in the class except Nate." He stood up. "I'd better get back to Nate." His gaze caught hers. "I really appreciate your coming to see about Nate's condition." He turned quickly, as if embarrassed by the intensity of his voice, and started away.

"Josh." Hallie's voice sounded loud in the small room. "I'll be here."

It was two hours before Josh returned.

"I didn't expect you to wait," Josh greeted her.

"Waiting rooms are interesting places," Hallie said, the lightness in her voice belying her weariness. "I've skimmed through magazines older than Nate, sampled coffee left over from last year, and met a lady waiting for her daughter to have a friendship ring removed from a swollen toe."

"That might endanger a friendship," Josh quipped without smiling.

Hallie felt her spirit lighten. She was glad to see a trace of humor, even if it was forced.

"Nate is awake. I thought you might want to say hello."

"Why don't I sit with him for a while. You could walk around, get a cup of coffee. But I'd suggest the cafeteria," she added.

"Maybe I will. Just for a few minutes. Sure you don't mind?"

Hallie assured him she didn't mind. She almost skipped down the hospital hallway to the room Josh had indicated.

Hallie stood beside the bed for a moment, gazing at Nathan's face in the subdued light. Dark lashes rested on smooth skin above his pale cheeks, and his bleached lips held only a tint of color. Feeling uncommonly maternal, Hallie longed to put the strand of hair falling across one closed eye back into place, but she stifled the urge. Slowly she lowered her body to the chair inches from Nate's bed and watched the soft rise and fall of his chest.

Shortly before midnight, after the shift change, a new nurse arrived to check on Nate moments after

Josh had returned from a second break, just in time to hear Josh mention that he hadn't found any coffee downstairs. She introduced herself and motioned them outside. "There's a fresh pot of coffee in the waiting room on this floor. I'll be with Nathan for a while, checking his vital signs and making an assessment. I understand his condition is improved, and I can see he is breathing well. Perhaps it's time for both of you to take a break. You might even go home and get some rest. Nathan will need your attention tomorrow."

She looked at them sympathetically. "I know how parents feel. I have two toddlers myself, and my husband and I are reluctant to leave them in the hospital without one of us nearby. But we do. We know one of us has to be alert the next day. So we draw straws."

Hallie rotated her shoulder, feeling the weariness tingle through her, and looked at Josh. In the harsh overhead lights of the hallway, lines of exhaustion surfaced around his eyes and mouth.

"Thanks," Josh said. "We'll try the coffee, but I think we'll pass on the straw thing."

The nurse tilted her head compassionately. "Try getting a little rest on the couch in the waiting room. I don't think we have many all-night visitors on the medical floor tonight."

Josh nodded and turned to Hallie. "Shall we?"

The medical floor waiting room seemed friendlier than the utilitarian plastic look of the emergency room. Two small lamps cast a restful glow across a mauve-and-blue-colored couch. Matching armchairs flanked a small table on another wall. Cups and a carafe filled a tray on a taller table.

Hallie watched Josh walk across the room to the large glass window and stare toward the touch of light piercing the towering pines. Emotionally worn herself, she wondered if Josh was trying to regain equilibrium by staring into the distance and letting the fear of the last few hours fade. She hoped, when he pulled his mind back to consciousness, that his outlook would be as sunny and calm as the start of a new day. She blinked and moved to the coffee tray. Lifting the carafe, she filled two cups with the aromatic liquid and carried them to the window.

Josh didn't turn his head. "The best treatment is prevention. Watching what Nate eats and breathes, knowing what triggers an attack and keeping him away from it." His voice was drained, as if remonstrating himself for the current trip to the emergency room.

Hallie set the cups on the nearby table. She knew he was in pain, pain beyond the reach of pills. Or her touch. Pain that would only ebb when he could accept Nate's improvement and realize he was out of danger—this time.

He turned slowly, facing her. She could see his eyes now, the worry lines harsh even in the dim light. She curled her fingers in her palms, attempting to squash the need to smooth the lines away with her fingertips.

"You can't know how much having you near meant to me."

"It's no more than the average, struggling substitute

teacher would do for her kindergarten class's room father."

"It's more than some mothers do."

Hallie's gaze searched his face, and he grimaced.

"Sibyl used to leave the hospital as soon as Josh was admitted to a room."

Hallie didn't have to ask if Sibyl had been his wife—it was obvious from the way he spoke. Sorrow wrenched at her heart. How could a mother leave her child and husband in such a crisis? Hallie lowered her gaze. She couldn't let Josh see her aversion to Sibyl's action. She shouldn't judge another person's reaction to a crisis. Maybe Sibyl could only cope by running. Still, she thought of Josh waiting alone in a friendless room.

"She said Nate was in good hands." Josh's voice was almost apologetic, as if defending Sibyl's defection.

Hallie breathed shallowly. The fingers that ached to feel the flesh of Josh's face could no longer be restrained.

She lifted one hand, sensitive fingertips touching his face, feeling the emerging stubble of overnight growth along his jawline. Her gaze touched his chin, his lips, his eyes.

She swayed, feeling as unsteady as a maple in a windstorm, and leaned toward him. She brushed against his chest and heard him breathe heavily. Involuntarily, she raised up on her toes and leaned forward to kiss the stubbled cheek. But Josh had turned slightly, and her lips touched his.

She pulled away, an odd feeling rippling through her, whirling her thoughts in circles like rolling hoops. She hadn't meant to touch him, let alone kiss him. It was just an outpouring of sympathy and concern. She struggled to calm her whirling thoughts, even as she raised glazed eyes to Josh.

Why couldn't she laugh lightly and tell him his coffee was getting cold and move away? Mentioning the kiss would make a big deal out of what was meant to be a casual gesture of compassion. But the look in Josh's eyes was not humorous or casual. The need Hallie felt was echoed in the depths of his eyes. She couldn't pull her gaze away from the mesmerizing look. She couldn't stare at the distant view of trees and water until her equilibrium returned.

She was helpless to move, even as his arms reached for her. She felt his hands on her arms, felt the heat of his fingers touch the bare skin beneath her short-sleeved blouse. The swaying-maple-tree sensation returned.

She shouldn't want this, but she did. She longed to feel his lips, even before he shifted his hands to her back, pulling her closer to him. She was aware that his right hand moved to cup the back of her head, aware that he bent his head toward her, aware of the scent of mint on his breath. Then she was lost in a whirl of sensation, wondering how the touch of lips could radiate through one's body with the speed of light. Embers, waiting to be stoked, flared into flames and spread like a conflagration through her body. She returned the kiss with a passion she'd never felt before.

When they pulled apart, Josh lowered his hands to her arms again. Holding her at arm's length, he looked into her eyes. He didn't have to say anything. It was as if they both remembered where they were and why they were here. He released her arms and turned away, looking toward the coffee carafe with unfocused eyes. "Did the nurse say there was some fresh coffee in here?"

Chapter Six

Pleasant memories of the waiting room and Josh's lips returned as sunlight, slicing through a slit in the bedroom drapes, woke Hallie. Then the recollection of why she'd been in that waiting room swept her warm, foggy thoughts aside with the force of a Santa Ana wind. She sat up and peered groggily at the hospital number she'd left on the telephone pad beside her bed. Instinctively, she lifted the receiver and dialed the number, but she pressed the disconnect button during the first ring. Just because she was awake didn't mean Josh and Nate were waiting for her call.

She peered at the clock on her bedside table, noting that it was after ten. She pursed her lips in indecision, then replaced the receiver. The call could wait until she was reasonably alert.

She'd left the hospital, reluctantly, in the early hours of the morning. With Nate's attack under control, Josh insisted he might sleep.

"You need rest, too, if you're driving to the city," he'd said.

But she hadn't been able to rest. It was dawn before the turmoil, roiling in her head like the wake of a motorboat on the lake, subsided. Pulling her body upright, Hallie cleared the remaining webs of sleep from her mind.

Even as she'd walked across the parking lot, she'd known Josh's words were a ruse to send her away from the anxiety-laden atmosphere surrounding Nate's bed. It was his way of getting her some needed rest. But at that moment, he'd crushed her.

She'd felt an ache of tenderness and compassion, familiar in her world of characters on paper, but rare in her daily life. She'd longed to hold him, to comfort him with her touch and soften the lines of fatigue creasing his face. She'd wanted to stay with him, to feel needed. Then his kiss had crossed the boundaries of comforting. It had evoked a feeling of exhilaration that soared above the distant mountain peaks, even as her toes tingled with the thrill of the flight. He'd sent her away while she was still trying to catch her breath.

She shelved the disturbing thoughts and shuffled to the bathroom. How could she have thought, even for a moment, that she could replace his wife?

Toweling dry after a quick shower, she returned to her room and rummaged in the closet for a clean blouse and pants. Josh had been considerate as usual. He'd known she was tired and remembered she had to drive to Los Angeles.

Her hand paused on a navy jacket. How could she

have forgotten the luncheon date with her agent? She glanced at the clock on her bedside table. If she called Josh now, she could then shower and change, and—with luck—she might make it to the restaurant on time.

Securing an oversized towel around her torso, she padded to the telephone and dialed, waiting expectantly for the sound of Josh's voice. An unfamiliar voice sounded in her ear.

Anxiety touched her before a reasonable thought suggested Josh had stepped out for coffee. But the woman who answered, who identified herself as the mother of a new patient in the room, said Nate's bed had been empty when her son was admitted.

Hallie pressed the disconnect button, redialed, and asked for the nursing station, worry clawing at her. Had Nate's condition worsened? Had he been transferred to the ICU?

A unit secretary answered, responding pleasantly to Hallie's question by saying she'd call the nurse assigned to Nate's care. Hallie murmured a word of appreciation and shredded a fingernail while she waited for the nurse. The pleasant voice sounded again, informing Hallie the nurse would be right with her. Hallie shoved her hand behind her to protect the tattered nail from further abuse. Finally the nurse answered, and Hallie identified herself as Nate's teacher.

"Nathan is improving," the impersonal voice said.

Hallie clenched the telephone. Improving, she thought wildly. Then why isn't he in his room? Where is his father? "He isn't in his room."

"He may be in X-ray. I can check."

Guilt touched Hallie. The nurse had assured her Nate was not in danger, and anyone could tell by the crispness of her reply that she had patients waiting.

"No, I'll call later," Hallie thanked the nurse and cradled the telephone. Josh would be with Nate.

Only partially convinced, she moved to open her lingerie drawer. The important thing was that Nate was improving. Before she'd left the hospital, Josh had reassured her again that the worst was over. She had to remember Josh was Nate's father; she was a substitute teacher—and right now, she was a screenwriter.

She confronted the mirror. This was the day for the power suit and the makeup she couldn't afford, but bought anyway. This was the time for a clear mind, eager and willing to absorb her agent's words—the time to keep worry about Nate under control. It was definitely the time to keep thoughts of Josh under control.

Pulling on a straight, somewhat short skirt, a buttoned blouse, hose, and high heels, Hallie went downstairs, the welcome scent of coffee banishing her early decision to leave immediately.

The aroma filtered from the kitchen, and Hallie realized with a sense of guilt that Lydia would want to know about Nate's condition. But Lydia wasn't in the kitchen.

Hallie poured coffee into a cup and carried it outside. She found Lydia Grant in the garden.

"Oh, you're up." The older woman looked up from

her weeding. "I heard you come in last night. Figured you'd sleep all day. How is the Snow child?"

"Improving when I left the hospital this morning." Hallie tasted the coffee. "The nurse said Nate was fine this morning." She lowered the cup, shrugging one shoulder. "Or words to that effect. They never tell you anything definite, do they?"

Lydia tapped her spade on the ground to release a clod of dirt. "If the nurse said he's fine, I'm sure he is." She peered at Hallie before looking back at the soil surrounding a clump of budding chrysanthemums. "I appreciated your call from the hospital last evening." She pressed the spade into the soil again. "You're a little dressed up for visiting the hospital."

Hallie peered at a chrysanthemum bud, the tight coils promising to blossom into butter-yellow petals. "I'm on my way to lunch with my agent."

Lydia nodded, removing her shoe-clad foot from the shovel. "Lunch?" She looked toward the sky.

Hallie grimaced. "I'm running late." She drained the cup, waggled it in the air, and turned back to the glass door.

"Safe trip," Lydia said.

After leaving a message for her agent that she might be late, Hallie called Nate's room again. Josh answered, and she clung to the sound of his voice, talking about Nate, the hospital, her trip to L.A., and Lydia's concern until she knew she had to leave. "I'll call after lunch with my agent," she promised.

She disconnected, telling herself she was going beyond the bounds of a substitute teacher's concern for a student. She closed her eyes in momentary frustration, unable to deny that her concern for Nate was heightened by her underlying desire to hear Josh's voice.

It was nearly three when Hallie parted with her agent. The restaurant was elegant, the food had been beautifully served, and she'd noted two celebrities at a nearby table.

Weaving her way through the sidewalk traffic, she walked briskly to her car, her thoughts tumbling. Her friend wouldn't be home until four, so she had time to call Josh. She wondered if the trip home with Nate was uneventful—if Paul had stayed to help him—if he'd had time for breakfast, or lunch? She'd eaten very little at lunch, as she listened to her agent's suggestion for changes in the script. Yet her mind kept straying back to the mountains, back to Josh—and Nate. She paused at the car door, keys in hand, hand on the door handle, and waited for a Lexus to pass. In the background, the crunch of tires on the asphalt penetrated her thoughts no more than the parade of shoppers and strollers on the sidewalk. Traffic moved, motors hummed, people laughed, and Hallie stood still. She didn't insert the keys in the slot. How could she stay in the city when her thoughts were in the mountains? She longed to hear Josh's voice, and a call inquiring about Nate wasn't enough.

With only a fleeting sense of guilt, she retraced her steps to find a telephone, leaving a message on Candace's answering machine, then redialing before she could change her mind, to tell Josh she was coming to cook dinner. With a brief stop at a nearby bakery, she was on the freeway by three-twenty.

Repressing a yawn, Josh focused on the customer and directed her to the canned corn. He'd slept a few hours in the chair beside Nate's bed after Hallie left. Sleep was difficult, with his thoughts of the beautiful teacher threatening to topple his emotional equilibrium.

Knowing she was going to the city, he'd still felt a stab of disappointment when she'd called to confirm her departure. His disappointment abated somewhat when she said she'd call later in the day.

Bringing Nate home from the hospital and dealing with a steady stream of customers kept Hallie out of his thoughts until she'd called this afternoon. Her voice produced an irrational increase in his pulse rate, and the anticipation welling inside him each time the door opened was embarrassing.

It was still hard to believe she'd stayed all night at the hospital with him, her presence offering support and encouragement—a different support and encouragement than the usual professional concern of medical personnel. Common sense told him her kiss was offering more support, more sympathy, but it had sparked a desire that had been smoldering in him for weeks. He shouldn't have succumbed, shouldn't have given an inch to the start of something that couldn't survive his problems. He tried to blame his lowered resistance on the long, tense hours of waiting beside Nate's bedside. With the relief of seeing Nate's thin, youthful chest relax, his breathing eased.

Sibyl would have left Nate in the emergency room, fleeing with relief when the doctor said Nate would be admitted. But Nate's teacher stayed to share the watch by Nate's bed, with obvious concern. She was a special lady, which he could have told her, adding a respectable and heartfelt handshake. Instead, he'd kissed her and sent his emotional world reeling.

He focused gritty eyes on the customer again, totaling her purchases and bagging them methodically. Two more customers entered and strolled the aisles with familiarity. Josh stretched and reached for an open can of cola.

She hadn't mentioned the kiss when he'd spoken to her on the telephone. Why would she? But something in her voice told him she had no more forgotten it than he had.

The thought brought mixed feelings. She was coming to cook, and he had to remember that was all. It wouldn't be easy with the memory of her lips melded against his. He wanted more than a memory, much more, which wasn't possible. She was special, but even if she could stay in the mountains, was she special enough to stay with him? Or would she leave him, in time, as Sibyl had?

At six o'clock, Hallie carried two bags into the country market, relieved to find no customers. Josh came forward, chuckling.

"You shopped somewhere else?" He indicated her bags with a grin. "How can I make a living if my friends don't support me?"

She smiled, a feathery, floaty feeling stealing through her. "How's Nate?"

"He was asleep when I looked in last. Paula—Paul's mother—is with him." He reached for the bags, sniffing the air. "Ah, fresh bread."

"The baker just took it out of the oven." She imitated his earlier chuckle. "Just a few hours ago."

"Smells great." He peered in the other bag. "What else?"

"A packaged salad. Fresh herbs. Basil, marjoram, a clove of garlic, and mushrooms." She waggled a hand in the air. "I didn't think you stocked fresh herbs or have mushrooms growing in the basement, so I stopped at the supermarket before starting up the mountain."

"Not many of the campers are looking for fresh herbs." Josh moved back to the counter and lowered the bags.

Hallie followed him, her gaze running over the shape of his head, the broadness of his shoulders. It was wonderful to be back in the mountains. "The one thing my aunt taught me to cook is spaghetti with Bolognese sauce. But she calls hers tomato sauce." Hallie laughed, unable to contain the joy bubbling inside her or to stop talking. "A can of tomato puree with salt and pepper—plus hamburger, if we could afford it. I've added ingredients. I cut a recipe from the paper and thought I was a gourmet cook when I bought half a dozen jars of herbs and spices. I left them with a neighbor when I moved this time, since I didn't expect to cook much."

Josh turned to face her, his eyes reflecting an inner glow. "I'll bet you even bake your own bread on occasion."

The bubbles rose in Hallie's chest, threatening the rhythm of her breathing and she wondered if her smile looked as airborne as she felt.

"I did price one of those breadmaking machines."

"A woman after my own heart."

Hallie's breath stalled.

Josh laughed self-consciously. "I mean, I thought you were a dedicated career woman. This is a side of you I'll have to get used to." He moved behind the counter. For a moment, only the sound of the refrigerator motor hummed along the aisles of the country market.

Hallie breathed carefully. Josh hadn't made a break for it, but he'd put a counter between them. "Don't get too used to it. I gave the seasonings away and didn't buy the bread machine."

Josh realigned the bags before he looked up. "You know, you're going to spoil Nate. He thinks spaghetti comes in cans and gets heated in a microwave."

"I can do that," Hallie retorted.

"After you've dangled the promise of gourmet cooking before me?" His eyes sparkled.

Grinning, Hallie tilted her head. "All right. Don't panic. I can't afford to buy herbs and not use them."

"So what else do you need before you change your

mind? Spaghetti, I know." He came around the counter and walked briskly to a nearby shelf.

"I'll need tomato sauce or puree." She watched his progression along the aisles. Not exactly running, she told herself dryly. But not strolling along with her at his side, either. She called out other ingredients, and minutes later he appeared, juggling the items. "Does this recipe call for meatballs?"

"It can."

"We stock frozen meatballs. Nate likes them."

"Do you have hamburger, maybe a little sausage?"

"We have."

"An onion?"

"Right. Anything else?"

"I forgot to buy green peppers," Hallie moaned.

"That's going to ruin the whole sauce?"

"No." Hallie added Josh's load to the spice bag. "It's just that I forgot them." She lifted the bread, but Josh reached for the heavier bag.

"I need to go upstairs to show you how to work my cantankerous stove."

Hallie looked toward the front door. "What if a customer comes in?"

"That's why I have a bell over the door." Josh stepped back, giving her ample room to precede him.

She moved past him. The intimate moment in the waiting room hadn't relaxed the kindergarten dad's wariness.

Upstairs, Josh introduced Paula and Hallie. Paula acknowledged the introduction with a warm smile, as did Hallie. She liked the older woman's open, friendly face immediately.

"Nate dropped off to sleep again while I was reading to him," Paula explained. "I worried that if he sleeps now, he won't go to sleep at bedtime, but I didn't have the heart to keep him awake." She turned to Hallie and asked about the drive to the city.

Hallie shook her head. "I used to think traffic leaving the city was heavier on Saturday. But I've been proven wrong lately. Going in is getting worse. Still, traffic moved steadily. No accidents or closed lanes."

Paula reached for a bag. "Can I take that for you?" She carried the bag, talking as she moved to the kitchen counter. "I miss the hustle and bustle—the club activities, the community things, the theater, lunching and shopping with my friends." Placing the bread on the counter, she turned. "But I'd never admit it to my husband. He enjoys the quieter life here so much." She turned to Josh. "Do you want me to watch the store for a while?"

Josh nodded. "If you would. I won't be up here long."

Hallie watched the trim, older woman, with her casual haircut and cheerful attitude, walk away, thinking she liked the lady. Josh must, too, or he wouldn't trust her to watch his son, even though he was only a few steps away.

Hallie followed Josh to the stove. He explained, "Two burners work fine. But one needs a new heating unit and this one"—he pointed to a rear burner—"needs special attention." He demonstrated a jiggling technique for unsticking the sluggish dial. Seconds later, the plate turned orange and Josh grinned proudly. "All in the fingers," he said breezily.

"I'm supposed to remember which way you jiggled." Hallie peered at the dial with cheerful skepticism.

"I plan to get a new one someday. Dial, not stove," he added. "Meantime, I practice patience."

From seeing him with his son, Hallie thought, he had more patience than many men. "I think my best bet is to leave the burner on until I'm through cooking."

Josh moved away from the stove, maneuvering to avoid brushing against her in the confined quarters. He stooped to rummage in a low shelf, extracting a limited selection of pots for her approval. "You know where the dishes are, I think." He straightened. "Any questions before I leave?"

"I'll think of them after you go," she said, wishing he would stay.

"Then I'll check on Nate." He still didn't move away. "Uh, if you need anything, I'm just downstairs."

Hallie nodded, watching him walk slowly across the room, unaccountably pleased at his reluctance to leave.

She filled a large pan with water and placed it on the orange-colored burner. She reached for the tomato sauce and now she had a question. Where was a can opener? She shook her head. That was not a good reason to call Josh.

The electric can opener was in plain sight—so much for a reason to get Josh back upstairs. She raised the can to meet the opener. Getting involved with Josh had not been her intention. She was a teacher concerned about one of her students. That she was attracted to his father was secondary. But somehow in the days following their meeting, concern and attraction had become something more.

True, she'd been thrilled when Josh showed an interest in her. Interest from an attractive man had assuaged the words of her former boyfriend. She lowered the open can. Interest was all right, but not emotional involvement. Anything between her and her adorable student's father could only be a summer fling—well, a post-summer fling. But today, or was it last night, a "fling" no longer seemed enough.

It was irrational to leave Hollywood and return to the mountains when she could have stayed to network. But the jubilant feeling that erupted when she'd walked in the store and saw the look of welcome in Josh's eyes banished any trace of guilt. It could be attraction—it *was* attraction. So maybe it was the comfortable, teasing talk, as if they were longtime lovers, that bothered her. She lifted a knife to dice celery and glanced over at the couch where Nate slept. His childish face was immobile, except for steady, normal breathing. Hallie turned back to her task.

The panic when Nate's breathing had become difficult at school and their shared watch at the hospital had brought them closer. But perhaps the hospital incident only reminded Josh of his wife. Had the kiss been an embarrassment, a feeling by him that he'd betrayed his wife in some way?

She found plates, salad bowls, and silverware, and set the table. She checked on Nate, then strained the spaghetti, ladled the sauce into a bowl, and prepared the salad. She inspected the table, and then wondered if Josh took his food downstairs to eat. She checked on Nate again and walked downstairs.

Josh was alone when she entered the room. "Spaghetti is ready."

"I could smell the sauce from here." He touched his tongue to his lip and sighed. "Paula will be right back to watch the store while we eat, though we don't get a lot of customers at this hour." He stepped toward the opening. "We don't have to wait for her."

"Nate's still asleep," Hallie said, as they walked upstairs.

"We can let him sleep. Spaghetti can be warmed in the microwave."

Hallie nodded, stopping at the top step at the sound of the bell.

"Paula?" Josh called.

At an affirmative answer, Hallie stepped onto the landing, moving to the table as Josh went to look at Nate.

"No paper plates?" Josh teased when he sat down.

"Special occasion," Hallie said.

"Yes, it is." His look indicated her presence was the special occasion.

Hallie flushed. "I meant Nate's recovery, his coming home from the hospital."

"That, too." Josh grinned, not dismissing his earlier meaning. He closed his eyes, lifted his head, and sniffed the air with a murmur of satisfaction. "Smells even better up here."

Hallie slid the spaghetti dish toward him, following it with the sauce. "Try the sauce while it's hot."

She watched him wind the spaghetti strands on his fork and lift it to his mouth. She glowed at his look of pleasure. The actor had scarcely noticed what she served, she thought, piercing a lettuce leaf with her fork.

"You must be exhausted. Did you get any sleep?"

"A few hours after you left."

Josh asked about her meeting with her agent and told her about his afternoon in the store. He raised a palm to answer Hallie's query about another helping. "The food was marvelous and the company even better. Thank you for both."

"I thought you had spaghetti often."

"Canned." He made a face. "No comparison with yours."

Hallie stood up, reaching for his empty plate.

"Don't do the dishes," Josh said. "I have to feed Nate, if Paula doesn't feed him. I'll do the dishes later."

"I'll rinse the plates." Hallie carried them to the sink. Unaware Josh had followed her, she turned as he reached to place the salad bowls in the sink.

For a moment, they looked at each other, Hallie aware of his body touching hers, of the warmth building within her. She wondered if the same feeling had invaded Josh. Was he thinking of the waiting room at the hospital in the early hours of the morning?

"Hallie, about last night."

"Yes?" She knew he was going say it couldn't mean anything between them, but she wanted him to say it, to tell her he couldn't forget his wife. Somehow it was better to be rejected because he couldn't forget his wife than the rejection she'd suffered when her boyfriend had told her she wasn't marriage material.

"You were wonderful to come to the hospital. To stay with Nate. With me. It's been a long time since I had anyone to share my concern about Nate. I was grateful."

"And you kissed me because you were grateful?"

"Not exactly." He didn't move away.

"Not exactly, what does that mean?"

"It means I care about you. But I can't get involved with you."

Despite the emotions bubbling inside her like an awakening volcano, was she any more ready to become involved than he was? Her heart said she was. But her head was reminding her she would return to the city soon.

"Nate is my sole concern. I have little left to give to any woman."

Hallie looked at him and saw pain in the depths of his eyes. She pressed one hand on the rim of the sink. The stainless steel felt as cold as the lump settling in her chest. What had she expected?

"I'm glad I could be there. I care about Nate." I care about you, too, she thought. But how could she tell him? "I know I can't replace the love his mother gave him. But I care. I know you must think of . . . of your wife every time you look at Nate—even more when he's ill. I know it's difficult to think anyone would care for Nate like his mother did, but I"—she hesitated—"I love Nate."

The sound from Josh's throat seemed to pierce Hallie's chest. Hallie pressed her palm against the chilly metal. Now she'd made things worse. Why couldn't she have just enjoyed this evening with Josh? Instead, she'd reminded him of the one person who should be here beside him.

"Sibyl found it difficult to cope with Nate's illness." The barest note of bitterness tinged his words.

"But you manage." Compassion softened Hallie's voice.

Josh nodded somberly. "That's part of being a parent."

Hallie couldn't pull her gaze away from his sober look, or forget the echoing touch of bitterness in his voice. "It's understandable if a part of you blamed your wife for dying and leaving you to cope."

"Dying?" His voice turned dry. "Sibyl was alive and well when she left us. The last I'd heard, she'd remarried."

Chapter Seven

Josh turned to cross to the window, staring into the distance as he had at the hospital. "Fact is, she seemed as happy as she did on *our* wedding day."

Hallie remained at the sink, a distant part of her mind grateful for the support. Vaguely she noted the sun no longer splashed through the windowpane. The room had darkened. She looked at Josh's back, confusion clouding her gaze. She wanted to shake her head or blink her eyes or do whatever it took to clarify the words echoing in her mind. Sibyl, Josh's wife, Nate's mother, wasn't dead.

Confusion clogged her ability to speak as well. The memory of a perfect wife and mother wasn't the problem! But this new knowledge didn't arouse a feeling of euphoria. She glanced at the sleeping kindergartner, then moved to stand beside Josh. The boulder blocking her vocal cords shifted minimally, allowing a few words to spill into the air before she could edit them.

"It's difficult to understand how"—she cleared her throat—"any mother could leave her child. But your wife must have had a good reason."

Josh turned his head, gazing at Hallie in silence. He inhaled, releasing the air slowly, his eyes dimming with each small, puffing sound. "Nate is not Sibyl's child."

His words tumbled in Hallie's head like clothes in a dryer. "You were married before Sibyl?"

Josh shook his head. "Nate is adopted."

Adopted. The spin cycle in Hallie's brain slowed.

"The adoption wasn't final when his asthma worsened. Sibyl wanted to return him to the agency, but I felt he was already ours. How could we send him away, not knowing who would care for him. He was our son. Our responsibility."

Compassion filled Hallie's heart. She wanted to touch him as she had in the hospital waiting room, to hold him and let him know someone cared.

"Sibyl isn't a bad person. I didn't realize how much she had to contend with. I worked long hours." He paused, his gaze turning toward the window. "I should have known. She tried to tell me in her own way. I thought making more money was the solution. She could hire help. But it didn't work out that way."

Hallie's gaze followed Josh's briefly, noting a lone boater guiding his small craft toward the wooden pier. She drew her look back to the man beside her, her heart swelling with admiration. How could he bear to speak well of the woman who'd deserted him and his son? Was it any wonder that his trust in others had been shattered?

"She left the following year, and I sold the business to my partner and moved to the mountains. Nate is improving and we're doing okay." He nodded, as if reaffirming his statement.

Hallie swallowed. "Yes, you are. You're a great father." She paused, giving herself time to strengthen her voice. "And a pretty good kindergarten dad."

Josh grinned weakly. "I did bug out before the party was over, but I warned you."

The earlier grimness of his voice faded, to Hallie's relief. She moved to the table, lifting the spaghetti and sauce bowls. "Things worked out okay. Marianne was there to help, and Lydia came as soon as she was notified. Substitutes are valuable people."

"Yes, they are." His look emphasized whom he was referring to.

Hallie's cheeks warmed. She carried the dishes to the counter. "Shall I put these in the fridge?"

"Leave them on the counter. Paula can wake Nate and feed him when she comes upstairs." Walking to pull a falling blanket over his son, he lingered to watch his breathing.

Hallie looked away before Josh could turn and catch her sharing his vigilance. "Will do," she said brightly. She pulled a roll of plastic wrap from a drawer where she'd seen it earlier and covered the bowls.

How could Josh blame himself because his wife had not been able to care for their ailing child? *Their* child. That Nate was adopted did not seem relevant to Hallie.

She remembered how Josh had said his wife's name
... *Sibyl.* She couldn't think of her as Nate's mother
now. Sibyl hadn't wanted him if he wasn't flawless.

Behind her, footsteps sounded on the polished floor.
She pushed the bowls aside, her look seeking a report
on Nate's condition. Josh's relaxed face answered her
silent query before he spoke.

"He seems fine."

Hallie smiled and looked away. She should go now:
she had no further reason to stay. Words of parting
stalled on her lips. She looked toward the table near
the staircase. Her purse was on the table, but where
had Josh hung her jacket? Ask him, she prompted herself. Say 'bye, pick up your purse, and go. She took
a breath, raised eyelashes that felt coated with lead,
and looked at Josh without speaking.

He rubbed one hand along the seam in his trousers,
nodding in the direction of the broad window. "We
could have coffee on the balcony."

Josh's voice flowed across the space between them,
warm and enticing, like the promise of a cozy fire on
a brisk autumn day.

Her reply hung in her throat. I'm trying to say good-
night here, she reminded herself. I'm trying to leave
gracefully, when all I want to do is stay and do the
dishes and sit with Nate and wait for you to come
home from work. She looked down at her short skirt
and high heels. Those kinds of thoughts didn't coin-
cide with living in Studio City. "Balcony?" Hallie repeated Josh's word to still the turmoil that flashed
across her mind.

Josh walked across to push back the drapes near the window, which exposed a door. "It may be a little breezy, but it's sheltered on one side."

"I noticed it, but I thought it was the door to your back stairs." Hallie said.

"It is. It's also a little balcony where I have coffee sometimes after Nate is asleep." He breathed out heavily. "I could use a cup of coffee before I go back downstairs."

Hallie's plan to leave wavered. She nodded her head, even as her words about leaving formed on her lips. She was unable to suppress the smile that spread across her face.

"Okay." Josh strode to the cabinet to lift the Thermos carafe from the coffee maker.

She watched him fill two mugs with dark liquid, aware she was more than attracted to him. But he had good reason to fear commitment in a new relationship, even if he was attracted to her. And he was. There was no doubt in her mind. But his control was formidable. Whether it was Sibyl's betrayal or his commitment to Nate, the barriers he'd built around his emotions were sturdy. Watching him turn and walk toward her, her heart gave a little lurch. For a moment, the thought rose in her mind that she'd like to show him all women weren't the same.

She opened the door, waiting for him to carry the mugs outside. Dry pine needles nested in the green plastic chairs pushed against the wall of the small balcony. A matching plastic table held a lone brown mug.

"Leave the door open," Josh said, pushing the mug aside to place the filled cups on the table.

Hallie pushed the door open again, knowing Josh needed to listen for any sounds from Nate.

He brushed the needles from the chairs. "I doubt if both chairs have ever been used. Paula is about the only one, besides Nate and I, who comes upstairs."

A ripple of pleasure touched Hallie, followed by a feeling of guilt. Someone to talk to, to share a cup of coffee with after a long day, wasn't asking much of life, was it? She risked a glance at his face. He wouldn't let it show, but his nights must be lonely.

"I forgot to leave a light on." Josh's voice was apologetic. "Just be a minute. Okay?"

"Sure." Hallie lifted her coffee cup to her lips. Maybe his nights weren't lonely. Maybe Nate's presence pushed back the shadows of loneliness for Josh.

But she didn't have a little boy. She shook the thought away. Pessimism had been crossed out of her dictionary. She'd learned years ago that crying didn't help. Maybe that's when she'd turned to creating friends on paper. Filling in the lonely hours of her youth with make-believe characters while her aunt was at work had sustained her through a loveless childhood. A twinge of guilt touched her, as if she'd been unfair to the aunt who had fed her and given her a place to live after her mother died. But there'd been no touching, no loving arms to hold her when she was frightened or ill. Involuntarily, she thought of the actor. Had she clung to him because she needed someone? Had their relationship failed because it was superficial? She tilted her head. Perhaps superficial was good. She hadn't been devastated when he'd deserted her.

She leaned her head back and gazed at the darkening sky. Superficial had been okay. It hadn't interfered with her career, her writing. But was she ready for this unusual feeling that permeated every pore of her body when she was with Josh, a feeling that smoldered unbidden when she was away from Josh?

Like a novice daring to undertake a perilous adventure, was she afraid to love because she'd never been loved?

She took a sip of coffee, waiting for Josh to return, storing away the thought that she was the woman Josh had invited to his balcony.

Aware of a lane of light spreading across the balcony, Hallie turned her head toward the open doorway with a sense of expectancy when Josh stepped onto the balcony.

"Coffee okay?" Josh lowered his body into the plastic chair nearest the doorway.

"Great," Hallie murmured. Her gaze swept over him slowly, noting the weary droop of his shoulders. Even tired, he looked good.

Josh reached for his mug and settled his shoulders against the high back of the chair. "Nate turned over. I waited to see if he was going to wake up."

A sudden brisk breeze swept across Hallie's bare arms, and she pressed her fingers against the warm surface of the ceramic cup. Beyond the balcony, pine needles rustled cozily, releasing their fragrance to enhance the evening air. Despite the cool air, Hallie gazed at the darkening view of towering pines and distant water with a feeling of contentment.

Beside her, Josh shifted, and she turned slightly to watch him sip coffee. Then he lowered his cup and made an indistinct noise, like he was clearing his throat or making a decision. Hallie looked away. Don't spoil the moment, she pleaded. You don't have to tell me there is no room in your life for me, nor remind me that I'm returning to the city.

"I thought I'd take Nate to ride on the Palm Springs aerial tramway when I'm sure he is better. Sort of make up for the party he missed and the time in the hospital."

A sense of relief touched Hallie. He wasn't going to mention the city or resign as room father or take Nate out of her class. She lifted her cup, taking a swallow of the cooling liquid. "Sounds like a good idea."

"I'm just thinking about it. I haven't taken Nate on any extended day trips."

Hallie lowered the mug. Should she tell him she knew how he felt? She hesitated.

Josh drummed his fingers on his cup. "I thought I might invite Robby to go along. Nate would have more fun if he had a friend his age with us."

Hallie made no comment. Being a substitute kindergarten teacher didn't equip her for giving advice or approval on an aerial tramway trip for a juvenile asthmatic. Being attracted to the father of the child made her even less of a candidate for rational thinking.

"I haven't approached Marianne with the idea, but if Nate had an asthma attack, I'd have a problem."

"Yes." Hallie nodded in emphasis.

"I need another adult to go with us, don't you think?"

So ask Marianne, Hallie said silently, angry at the touch of feeling she knew was jealousy. She lifted her cup and sipped cold coffee. Below the serenity of the pine-scented balcony, the sound of a car traveling over the gravel road from the campgrounds sounded. A breeze ruffled her hair, and she reached to sweep it off her forehead. "Probably," she said calmly.

Josh was silent for a time, and Hallie wondered if he was listening for a sound from Nate.

"I know you see children all week and you have plans in the city on the weekends, but . . ." He hesitated, and Hallie's breath slowed. "Maybe you'd like to go along?" he said in a rush. "Nate would like it," he added.

He was asking her to accompany him and Nate and Robby on this first all-day outing with his son.

"I'd like it, too," Hallie said, realizing she meant it more than she expressed. Inside, an irrational, ridiculously humorous voice was giggling . . . he hadn't been thinking of Robby's mother.

"Good." Josh sounded relieved. He drained his cup and stood. "I should relieve Paula."

"I know." Hallie stood, wondering how her voice could sound so calm when everything inside of her was dancing and singing and daring anyone to rain on her parade.

She forced her mind back from whatever outer space she'd flown to and took her cup inside to the counter. Turning, she looked for Josh, preparing with difficulty to bid him a polite good-night before she fled to examine her feelings.

Her gaze found Josh standing near the couch where Nate slept. She crossed the room to stand beside Nate. For a moment, watching the almost imperceptible movement of the blanket covering Nate's chest, she felt they were together, floating in a rainbow-hued soap bubble. Then Josh moved, his business persona returning.

"I should get back to the store."

Flustered, Hallie managed a sociable good-night. She retrieved her purse and jacket, responded to Josh's thanks for the dinner, and hurried down the stairs, glad Paula was busy with a customer. She hurried to her car.

"It's been two weeks since Nate's asthma attack," Paula said firmly, after Nate had gone upstairs to put his backpack away. "He brings up the tram trip almost every day. He's not going to forget about it. You could use some time off. And"—she hesitated for emphasis—"I believe the tram shuts down at the end of October."

"I know." Josh moved to take over her stocking chores. "I called."

"Well?"

"This weekend. I'll ask Hallie if this Saturday is okay for her." He removed two cans and slid them into an empty space on the shelf in front of him. "First, I should ask if it's okay with you."

Paula laughed. "I'm glad to get out of cooking and cleaning at home. This Saturday is fine. Paul will be back from his medical checkup by then, and he'll help."

"Thanks, Paula. I'll talk to Hallie when I pick up Nate."

He turned back to the shelves. Yes, he had to talk to Hallie. About more things than the trip to the tramway. He should resign his position as room father for the kindergarten classroom. He knew, with every passing day, that he was putting off the inevitable. Keeping his sanity depended on seeing less of Hallie.

Inviting her on the tramway trip might have been a mistake, but he'd been vulnerable that day. He'd stalled last weekend. Seeing Hallie five days a week, when he picked up Nate, was eroding the wall he'd erected against emotional involvement. He needed a friendly, nonemotional relationship with a woman, a woman who would love his son and accept him. He lifted more cans. He'd talk to her today and set up the trip. Then he could ask her to look for a new kindergarten dad.

The October sun had cast a pale light through the window when Hallie first turned on the computer. Her Cindy Ellen was no *Pretty Woman*, but her role was shaping up—until the telephone rang.

Now, nestling the telephone between her left ear and her shoulder, she listened to her friend's voice.

She'd been awaiting the call with some dread, ever since she'd left a message on Candace's answering machine.

"Hallie," Candace wailed. "This party Saturday evening is important. Getting an invitation for you wasn't easy. An independent producer will be there who is looking for writers with fresh ideas."

"I know," Hallie murmured. Guilt singed her throat.

"You're going to miss the meeting, too." Hallie could hear the deep sigh of exasperation as clearly as if her friend sat across the room. "You can't expect your agent to do everything, you know."

"Candace, I'm sorry. Really. I know you went to a lot of trouble. You're a wonderful friend." She took a steadying breath. "I made this commitment to a student."

"Another one!"

Hallie stared at the light on the computer screen. "No. The same one."

"The asthmatic?"

Hallie winced. Candace sounded like the nurse at the hospital who labeled people in terms of their illness instead of their names. "Yes," she acknowledged. "His name is Nate."

"Nice name. And he sounds like a nice kid." The voice on the receiver was silent for a second, and Hallie could imagine Candace suppressing her irritation before she spoke again. "I hope this date with him is important enough to forgo what might be your big break."

Hallie felt her mind churning. She didn't know if

she was doing the right thing . . . so maybe she should cancel the trip with Nate and Josh. Opportunity might just be waiting for her to walk in the room while she was miles away traveling toward the top of a mountain.

"Candace," she said with a touch of resignation, "we've been trying to find that big break at every party and conference we attend. I've got to believe this party isn't as important as going with Nate."

Hallie could tell by the *whoosh* of sound reaching her ear that her friend wasn't convinced. "Couldn't Nate's father take him next weekend, or for that matter, any other weekend?"

"Not really. This trip is kind of a makeup for the party Nate missed when he had to go to the hospital. Josh, that's Nate's father, wants to take Nate while the weather is still mild."

"I know who Josh is." Candace laughed dryly. "You've mentioned him more than once. Are you sure he isn't the reason you're going on this trip?"

Hallie paused, hearing the soft hum of the computer in the quiet room. She didn't answer the question, even to herself. "Candace, I know it's hard to understand, but Nate's last attack occurred because of something he ate in my classroom. So when Josh asked me and said he'd invited another child and he'd feel more comfortable if two adults went, just in case Nate has a problem, how could I refuse?"

"Knowing you, I guess you couldn't." An exaggerated sigh came over the wire. "You couldn't take the kids to Disneyland, or the Los Angeles zoo, and drive here later?"

"I don't think Josh would go for that. Disneyland maybe, but Josh seems hesitant to take Nate to Los Angeles."

"Why the tramway?" Candace's voice was resigned, almost as if she didn't expect an answer.

Hallie explained anyway. "While Josh was sitting with Nate at the hospital, he kept him entertained with tales about riding on the tram when he was younger. Naturally, Nate wants to ride on the tramway, too. So Josh promised to take Nate when he got better. You know kids. 'Someday' means right now."

"Have a good time," Candace said, her voice lacking spirit. "Call me next week."

"Will do." Hallie paused. "Candace, thanks again, even if I can't make it." Hallie lowered the receiver and turned back to the computer screen, her thoughts still on the conversation. She could still call Josh and beg off going on the trip, but she knew she wouldn't. She lowered her fingers to the keyboard. After staring at the print on the screen for twenty minutes without writing a single word, she glanced at the clock. She should get enough sleep to be alert tomorrow, she told herself. She closed the program and clicked the suspend button.

Chapter Eight

Marianne was leaving the parking lot as Hallie entered, and she lifted a hand. Hallie returned the wave and drove on to park at the side of the building. When she opened the door to the store, Josh loomed into view, lifting his head to let a broad smile break across his face. It was as if he'd been waiting for her, she thought joyfully.

He turned to speak, and two of Hallie's kindergarten moppets appeared from behind the counter.

"Miss Ember, Miss Ember, we've been waiting for you," Nate shouted.

Hallie's heart swelled. Thoughts of meeting someone in a production company who might read her script, or even an actor who saw potential in the character in her script, fled. The log lines she'd worked on, just in case she needed to tell her story in a few sentences, were filed away. Today was for Nate.

The drive down the mountain road to the freeway

was pleasant. Traffic moved steadily past a quiet university city and groves of citrus and avocado trees.

Their conversation was general, interrupted at times by Josh calling attention to something he wanted the boys to see. The scenery changed to the low-lying shrubs of the desert and a sparse scattering of houses. Further on, acres of towering concrete poles with whirling arms populated the land, and the boys watched in awe as Josh told them that the windmills of the desert captured the wind to generate power.

They arrived at the turnoff leading to the tram well before noon. Cars, vans, and various other vehicles filled the parking lot. Checking to see that the excited youngsters had their jackets, Josh closed and locked the doors. He eyed the incline leading to the tramway building warily. But he said nothing as the boys scrambled uphill, dodging adroitly around slower travelers. Hallie was puffing by the time they reached the first benches. Minutes later, she looked up to find Nate and Robby outside the doors to the building, waiting impatiently for their older companions to reach the entrance.

"Hurry up, Dad, we're gonna miss the tram," Nate wheezed softly.

The grin on Josh's face never wavered as his gaze lingered on his son, flicking from his excited face to his laboring chest. "If we do, there'll be another one."

Hallie admired his control. Wouldn't she have been rushing forward to peer lengthily at Nate's chest, insisting they go sit on the nearby bench and rest before continuing inside? But Josh held the doors open for the boys without comment, then waited for Hallie to enter before him.

Joining the throng of people inside, Nate and Robby forgot about the tram for more immediate adventures.

"Dad, can we look in the shop?"

Hallie glanced at Josh and saw an indulgent grin touch his lips. He peered at the gift shop, as if searching for escapees from a peanut farm, before he answered. "Don't see why not." He moved his head to catch Hallie's attention. "If you stay with Miss Ember while I see about the tickets." He lifted an eyebrow at Hallie, awaiting her approval.

Hallie nodded, pleasure touching her. Josh had come a long way since he'd warily stood in the doorway of the kindergarten classroom.

Josh reached a hand into his hip pocket, withdrawing a worn wallet, and extended a bill to each child. "No food," he said, then grinned to take the stern tone from his voice. "Let Miss Ember help you pick out a souvenir from the shop."

She trailed the boys into the shop, delighted over their awe at the treasures inside. Shopping with two inquisitive boys on a limited budget wasn't easy, she found, noting their money and the price of their selections. A glass globe housing two adults, a child, and a snowman amid a stand of pines called for a second look. She lifted the globe and turned it, her gaze following the fall of the snowflakes as they kissed the cheeks of the family of figures. She smiled dreamily, then checked the pricetag. She returned the globe to the shelf. Her budget couldn't be expanded to include such frivolous purchases.

Looking up, she caught a glimpse of Josh striding away from the gift shop and wondered if he'd remained to see that the boys were staying close to her. She glanced at the youngsters in her care. They were intent on examining a miniature action figure.

Minutes later, she knew that supervising kindergarten shoppers on a card-buying trip hadn't prepared her for this. Robby was halfway across the shop, chasing dinosaurs, before she could lift her eyes from a quick view of Nate's electronic gadget. With a calmness she didn't feel, she managed to get the two together, coax them into buying affordable souvenirs, and urge them toward the entrance by the time Josh returned.

"Any problems?" Josh looked at the boys as if he expected them to appear disheveled and puffing.

"None at all." Hallie grinned at her charges.

"Miss Ember's fun to shop with," Nate announced loudly.

"Yeah," Robby agreed enthusiastically. "She likes dinosaurs." He held up a miniature replica of the animal.

"And rangers, too." Nate displayed his treasure.

Josh bent to peer closely at the figures. "Bet you couldn't find these in our store in town," he said solemnly, glancing up at Hallie with a touch of amusement in his dark eyes.

"No way," Robby said.

Hallie grinned at the breezy phrase and moved closer to Josh as a press of people shuffled by. Giggling teenagers, oblivious of others, weaved rapidly through the throng. A young couple carrying two pre-

schoolers moved slower, heading in the same direction. All around her, couples, young and old, some
holding children, some holding hands, moved in a holiday atmosphere. Her gaze moved from the crowd to
Josh and Nate. This is what family life should be, she
thought, and a momentary ache for a life she'd never
known touched her. She'd lived in Southern California
all of her life and she hadn't ridden the tramway, or
gone on an outing that wasn't sponsored by the school.
She felt a twinge of guilt at her thoughts. Her aunt
worked overtime just to pay the rent. When she had a
day off, she was too tired to walk around an amusement park, she'd told Hallie more than once.

Beside her, Josh straightened. "Think you're ready
to take the dinosaur and the ranger on a tram ride,
guys?"

He waited for their combined nods before he turned.
"Ready for the big adventure, Hallie?" He reached to
take her hand.

The touch of the strong, slender fingers grasping
hers traveled far past her fingers. She nodded, lifting
her gaze to meet his. For a moment, they shared the
pleasure of being together, of being a part of the cheerful crowd. Then the look deepened. Hallie could sense
the need behind the change in Josh's eyes; it matched
her own. Then Josh pulled his gaze away, releasing
her hand. He turned to the boys. "The next car will
be here soon," he said. "We'd better get a move on."

Nate and Robby looked back at the intriguing shop,
then turned, eagerness relighting their faces.

"Okay," they chorused.

Josh guided them to the waiting area for the tram, slowing at the throng of people in front of him. Seeing the press of people, Hallie, too, held back, glancing at Josh with a thread of anxiety. Was he having second thoughts about taking Nate on the tram?

That would be a little redundant now. Canceling the ride for the excited youngsters would be unconscionable, wouldn't it? Josh would have to hope that none of the inhabitants of the crowded, enclosed car carried a cold or flu germ—or any of the other things that could cause a change in Nate's breathing.

The broad line ahead of them stopped, and Hallie looked down to check on Robby and Nate. When she looked up again, the red tram car appeared in the distance. Under a blue sky the gondola, suspended from a heavy cable, moved slowly over an imposing gorge far below. Hallie's gaze traveled to the towering construction of beams supporting the overhead cable with a touch of anxiety. But if the boys even noticed the distance between the gorge and the jolly red car, it didn't dampen their excitement.

The gondola creaked noisily to a halt, and the line of prospective passengers moved a few inches. The guide's voice sounded above the throng of people, instructing those at the front of the line to enter the waiting car. She moved, keeping the boys in front of her, aware that Josh was even more cautious. He laid one hand on the small shoulders of each youngster.

Shuffling to keep the boys near, Josh entered the car, maneuvering a place for them near one of the windows. He turned to look at Hallie, as if assuring himself she, too, was near, and a surge of warmth filled her at his concern. Then the crush of bodies moved, and her body touched his.

With a jolt, a screech of metal, and a mechanical groan, the gondola swung away from the platform. Minutes later, it soared upward, high above the massive chasm below. Aware Josh stood so close, his breath touching her cheek, Hallie concentrated on a vertical slab of granite rock. The granite was as smooth and marbled as if it had been carved by a master chef. The car swayed and Hallie steadied her stance, touching Nate's shoulder protectively. Almost at the same time, Josh's arm encircled her waist. Just his touch, even through layers of clothing, increased her pulse rate and warmed her heart. She caught herself before she leaned against him.

She tilted her head, lifting her gaze to meet Josh's. "I rode in an elevator with wall-to-wall people once. I was terrified that a power failure would leave us stranded between floors, and I promised myself I'd avoid elevators with more than four passengers."

Josh chuckled, a glint of humor in his eyes. "You can compare an elevator ride with this? Look at the view."

"Beautiful, isn't it?" *And no, riding in an elevator with strangers in no way compares to standing beside you in a gondola.*

The car slipped smoothly up the cable, and Josh's hand moved from her waist. She felt a sense of loss, then glanced aside to see that his hands were again touching Robby's and Nate's shoulders.

She focused on the gray-green bushes clinging determinedly to the slabs of granite a few feet away from the broad expanse of glass before her. In the background, a voice sounded over the speaker, and Hallie tried to hear the words through the din of voices around her.

The automated voice found its way to her in disjointed sentences. "Project started in the early 1900s ... Crocker, known as the father of the tramline ... took thirty years to complete ..."

"Dad, look." Nate's nearby voice overrode the announcer.

"What is it, son?" Josh bent to listen.

"It's gone. It was right there on that rock."

"... we've reached the halfway point. We're now passing the other car on its downward ..." the announcer continued.

Nate overrode the voice. "A little furry animal. But he ran away. Didn't you see him?"

"Maybe it was a raccoon. I hear raccoons, foxes, coyotes and bobcats, and even bighorn sheep are sometimes seen around here."

Hallie scanned the bleached rocks for bighorn sheep, eager to show Nate and Robby something different. But no animals appeared to please the tram riders. In the distance, atop a granite crag smoothed into a pedestal by time, stood a majestic fir, poised like a Christmas tree awaiting the decorative flakes of winter snow. Projections of plants Hallie couldn't name squeezed their foliage through cracks in the jagged rocks lining the path of the gondola. Then the gondola ground to a noisy stop and the passengers moved to exit. The boys bounced in their eagerness to start another adventure, but Hallie felt a faint reluctance to leave the closeness of the foursome.

"It's hard to believe we left the desert a little while ago and with a fifteen minute or so ride, we're high in the mountains," Hallie marveled.

"Do you want a cup of coffee or a soft drink before we go outside?" Josh indicated a snack bar.

"Not unless you or the boys want one." But the boys were already heading for the exit of the building.

Josh lifted his eyes heavenward. "I guess that answers my question." He turned to follow the boys. "Hey, guys, slow down."

The pair stopped, waiting impatiently while Josh stopped to look out from the terrace. A curving walkway led past boulders, a picnic table, and pines.

"Does it look the same as you remember?" Hallie asked.

"Not quite. It was the first or second week of March when I was here then. Snow covered the ground, and my friend and I plopped in the snow along the walkways and flapped our arms to make impressions of snow angels. We threw snowballs at each other and all the nonsense pre-teen boys do to show off." He grinned a little sheepishly. "There were a couple of girls watching us. I remember looking up and seeing Mom and Dad standing just about where we are and feeling kinda silly, but it didn't stop us."

Hallie took a breath of the crisp, cool air and looked down on the path below; she wished she had been one of the girls watching the boys show off. Then Nate moved closer and tugged his father's jacket. "Can we go down now, Dad?"

Josh nodded. "Don't get too far ahead of us."

Josh pointed off into the distance before they followed the boys. "Beyond the station, fifty-four miles of trails run through the mountain for adventurous hikers. There are also campgrounds." He paused and laughed. "Not the hookup to sewer and power kind, like the one behind the store, though. They're the roughin' it kind."

"I suppose you hiked all fifty-four miles."

"All but fifty-two or so. Dad said we had to get back before the last car down. Actually, I think he was getting tired."

Hallie pulled her gaze away from Josh. One could tell that his father had been a good role model. But Josh had improved on his role model. He was a good man, a good father, a good provider—and probably a good husband. But his wife's desertion had really deep-sixed his confidence about his ability to be a good husband now.

They stopped to watch a couple of gray squirrels scurry across the path, chasing each other like children, then pausing to raise their bushy tails as if posing for the visitors. Bright eyes stared from beneath furry brows at the onlookers. With a feeling of well-being, Hallie wondered if they were waiting for applause from the crowd. Tiring of their audience, the spirited animals scampered past a picnic table and benches to disappear into the trees.

The foursome walked on, the younger pair stopping to examine acorns and pine cones and fallen leaves. Half an hour later, they turned around and walked back to the station. They found an empty table at the restaurant and ate a light lunch. They looked through the telescope at the desert thousands of feet below the mountain station. Hallie relished every moment, not wanting it to end, yet knowing Josh wouldn't want Nate to become overtired.

It was midafternoon when Josh propelled the boys toward the lift to return to the valley station. The rhythm of Nate's breathing seemed no different than Robby's. He held his tongue as the pair scrambled toward the four-wheeler.

Inside the vehicle, he checked to see that the boys had fastened their seat belts. He'd enjoyed the day away from the store. He'd enjoyed it more because Hallie was beside him, he admitted. He changed gears and drove away from the valley station, turning on the highway leading to Palm Springs. "Anybody hungry?" His voice was teasing. He knew the answer. When weren't active boys hungry?

"We are," two voices chorused from behind him.

"How about you, Hallie? Something more substantial than the soft drink and thin sandwich we had for lunch?"

"I could eat," Hallie agreed.

"Hamburgers, Dad. Please." Nate pleaded.

"Hamburgers it is, but let's find a place that serves other things as well."

Entering Palm Springs, Josh drove along a one-way street, looking at the signs on the store fronts. He slowed down across from a blush-colored adobe building, signaling to turn into the parking lot. "This one has a nice patio with a view of the mountains."

Parking in the half-empty lot, he walked briskly around the front of the vehicle to open the door for Hallie. But she was already swinging her lithe legs toward the ground. The boys, too, had opened the sliding door and were scrambling from the vehicle. He breathed deeply. Life was good. Nate hadn't shown one sign of breathing difficulty. And it just felt right to be with Hallie.

He extended a hand to Hallie, and she took it and stepped down to the asphalt. The feel of her hand was warm in his, and he looked at her windblown hair and pink cheeks and bright, lively eyes and thought how beautiful she looked.

She released his hand and reached to grasp one small hand of each boy. "Could I just hold your hands until we get across this parking lot?" she asked solemnly. "There's a lot of cars turning in here. If we're all three together, they can see us better, don't you think?"

Josh watched the boys look at her uncertainly, but by then Hallie was walking steadily across the lot. She released their hands at the entrance to the patio. "Thanks for the escort," she said to the pair, and turned to Josh. "This is nice. Can we eat here?"

"Don't see why not. There are plenty of empty tables. The lunch crowd must have left hours ago, and it's early for the dinner crowd." He lifted a hand to touch her back and then pulled it away. It was becoming too easy for him to forget that he couldn't become romantically involved with her.

A shorts-clad waiter took their drink orders and left them perusing oversized menus.

Nate eyed the single-paged menu the hostess had placed in front of him. "Dad, do they have hamburgers here?"

Josh groaned good-naturedly. "Yes, they do, Nate."

The shorts-clad waiter returned with iced tea and soft drinks and asked if they were ready to order.

"You do make hamburgers?" Josh inquired, ignoring the variety of fanciful names listed on the menu.

"Will that be with french fries or oven fries?" he asked.

"An' ketchup," Nate blurted, looking at his dad for support.

"And ketchup," Josh affirmed. He didn't take Nate out to eat that often, so it must be the television commercials.

Josh glanced toward Hallie. She sipped iced tea, her gaze locked dreamily on the view of the purple mountain looming in the distance. She looked so entranced, so lovely, Josh hated to interrupt her reverie. But she turned, her beautiful eyes meeting his when he spoke her name and answered, as if she'd been aware of every word spoken at the table.

"Chicken salad."

"And you, sir?" The waiter's voice echoed in Josh's ear.

For a moment, Josh couldn't remember what he'd planned to order. Then reality kicked in, and he gave the waiter his order.

He glanced at Hallie when the boys squirmed and jostled, but she didn't seem to notice their antics. When the waiter returned with coloring place mats and a box of crayons for each child, and the boys bent over their coloring projects, Josh relaxed slightly. He was surprised to find he could lean back and join Hallie in watching strollers on the sidewalk beyond the low wall enclosing the patio. He was surprised to discover they could comment on the mild weather and the view of the magnificent mountains looming over the city . . . surprised he forgot for a moment to check on Nate's breathing.

The CLOSED sign was on the store when they pulled into the parking lot, and only Marianne's car gleamed in the glow of the overhead light spraying across the asphalt. With the boys beside her, silent for a change, Hallie waited for Josh to unlock the front door.

"Hope Marianne isn't upset with us," Josh said. He waited for Hallie and the boys to preceed him across the dimly lit store.

Hallie paused in the doorway of the rec room. Marianne didn't look upset. She sat on the couch in the cluttered room, holding a sleeping child in her arms and watching television with Paul. Her preschooler sat on Paul's lap.

But she was ready to leave, saying she needed to get the children in bed. Paul, too, bid them good-night, saying he'd give the preschooler a ride to the car. Josh thanked Paul for staying, and as Marianne and Paul left together, Josh looked at Hallie and grinned. "I don't think he minded, do you?"

"They look rather friendly," Hallie agreed, watching the couple travel to Marianne's car. "I think it's time I said good-night also."

Josh touched her arm. "Nate, say good-night to Miss Ember and go up and brush your teeth. I'll be up to check the brush in a minute."

Nate gazed at his teacher with sleepy eyes. "Goo'night, Miss Ember."

"Good-night, Nate. I'm so glad you wanted me to go on the tram trip. I had a good time."

"Me too," Nate said.

"Teeth," Josh repeated softly.

Josh watched his son until the door of the store closed behind him. Then he turned to Hallie.

"I had a wonderful day, Josh. Thanks for asking me."

"It wasn't like another working day for you, supervising kindergartners?"

"Not at all," Hallie denied vehemently.

"You wouldn't have rather been in Hollywood?"

"Where's Hollywood?" Her eyes widened.

"You're eyes are beautiful when you're teasing me."

Fireflies flitted across Hallie's line of vision. "Thank you, kind sir, for the compliment." She took a breath, anchoring her gaze to the collar of his shirt. "Thank you again for the trip." She tried to sound polite, but her voice softened. "Truly, I enjoyed the trip and the company."

Josh nodded. "My pleasure."

"I'd better get home so you can get Nate to bed."

She knew she should protest when Josh accompanied her to the car. Nate needed him. But she couldn't voice the protest. She didn't want Josh to leave. She wanted to prolong their time together as long as possible.

The overhead lights faded as they walked to the side of the building where Hallie had parked, and Hallie searched her purse to find her keys by touch in the semidarkness. She opened the car door, slid her purse across the seat, and turned back to Josh.

"See you at school," she said cheerfully.

Josh lifted a hand, dangling a small bag in the stream of light from the open car door. "I got you a small souvenir of our trip. So you won't forget."

Hallie looked up, surprised at the gift, and met a gaze that seemed intent on capturing hers. "As if I could."

She pulled her gaze away from the intense eyes. Untangling a ribbon tie, she separated the cords and pulled the bag open. Tissue paper covered the contents. She looked up at Josh, grinning self-consciously. "I'm getting there."

"More trouble than it's worth." Josh laughed, but Hallie could tell he was waiting for her comment. She pushed the paper aside and dipped a hand into the bag, feeling the smooth, silken slide of glass beneath her fingers. With both hands, she lifted a glass globe from the bag and realized she held the glass-encased family figures in the cup of her fingers. She rocked the globe and snow cascaded over the winter scene.

Her heart rocked, and she wondered if stardust could shimmer in one's chest. When had he seen her with the fanciful globe? Then she remembered his back as he walked away from the shop on his way to buy tram tickets.

"Oh, Josh, it's lovely. You didn't have to give me anything to remember the trip." She didn't look up. Even if it was semidark, he might see the moisture in her eyes. She cradled the globe in one hand and tried to lower it into the bag but the bag shifted and he had to help her. Securing the globe inside the bag, Josh leaned to set it behind the front seat, and then straightened. "Thanks, Josh. It's been a perfect day." She lifted a hand to touch his cheek, her fingers grazing the trace of stubble on his skin.

"I should thank you," Josh replied. "It meant a lot to Nate . . . and me."

Hallie could not control the urge to raise on her toes and touch her lips to his. It wasn't planned. Nor could she regret the surge of emotion that overcame her when Josh returned the kiss. He pulled her close, seeming to succumb to a need to feel her against him. She felt his hands on her shoulders and her waist, and she felt a flare of flame spread though her body. He'd pulled his lips away for a full minute before she managed to apply a brake to her spinning senses.

"I'd better see about Nate," Josh said huskily. His

hands raised to slide over her arms. But he didn't release her.

"Yes," Hallie agreed. Her voice was as filled with emotion as his. "Yes," she said a second time, managing to get the word out. She turned and slid into the front seat of her car.

Josh held the door open for a moment, his gaze holding her to him. "See you Monday," he said, and closed the door.

Hallie raised a hand and started the car. She drove away before he turned to go into the store.

She drove slowly, reliving the feel of his lips. She hadn't planned this. She'd only been concerned about Nate and his asthma, and she'd admired his father for caring for him alone. She'd thought she could help. She'd liked Josh, getting to know him as a caring father, a man who took his responsibilities seriously. When she'd discovered Josh's pain, she'd wanted to show him that not everyone wasn't to be trusted. When had she'd gotten in over her head? When had she fallen hopelessly in love?

Chapter Nine

Autumn appeared overnight in Southern California with an overcast sky and a drop in temperature. Television weather reports showed Texas towns awash in water and Alabama coastal residents securing windows and doors with the threat of an approaching hurricane. In comparison, the midday weather was as wonderful as Hallie felt. Josh was walking toward her when she'd gone to her car to retrieve a basket of autumn decorations for her classroom.

With Nate skipping ahead, Josh lifted the basket and eyed the contents. "Decorating the classroom today?"

"Later this afternoon."

"I can help when I return to pick up Nate."

"Return?" Hallie lifted an eyebrow.

"I need to pick up some things."

Hallie managed to suppress her surprise. He was trusting her with his son for an hour!

The afternoon session went so quickly, Hallie didn't

148

notice Josh hadn't returned by the time class was over. He returned as the children were leaving, snagging Robby at the door to lean over and speak to him. Robby whooped and ran to join Nate. Hallie smiled, glad to see the two had become good friends.

She saw the other students and Anna out, then returned to join Josh. "Did you finish your errands?"

"I did. With time left to help Paul in the store."

Hallie lifted an eyebrow. "So, are we ready to decorate the room?" She included Nate and Robby in her invitation, though she expected Robby's mother would be here soon.

"I think so." He looked down at the youngsters for a confirmation, then back to Hallie. "You have an extra helper today. I told Marianne I'd watch Robby. She's going to pick him up at the store."

Ooh. Hallie didn't look at Josh. "The more help, the merrier we'll work," she said cheerfully. Why shouldn't Josh and Marianne be friends? she asked herself fiercely. She lifted a basket of acorns, pine cones, and orange, gold, and brown paper leaves and carried it to the bank of windows.

Josh followed. "Marianne had a doctor's appointment for her youngest child."

Hallie nodded. "It's nice you could help."

"Marianne's a good lady. I don't know how she manages three youngsters by herself."

Hallie couldn't fault his admiration. She wondered if Marianne and Josh shared some of their problems when they met as they picked up their sons?

She lifted a red-gold leaf and held it up, her eyes

glazing past the colorful scrap of paper. "Babysitting. Next, you'll be car pooling." Her voice was light.

Josh tilted his head back and lifted his eyes upward. "Like I have time to car pool." His voice was cheerful, but Hallie thought she noticed a faint note of frustration. If the sound had been there, it vanished as the youngsters slid between them. Josh lowered his gaze to the jostling pair.

A prick of conscience bothered Hallie. He didn't have time to hang paper leaves in classroom windows or decorate pine cones either. She'd thought suggesting he volunteer as a room father would be a way for him to spend time at the school with his son. Or had she been thinking how nice it would be for *her* to spend time with Nate's father? Even today, she hadn't thought about what it was costing Josh to hire Paul to stay in the store while he played kindergarten dad. Money he could ill afford, her conscience nagged, considering Nate's medications and medical bills.

But he was here. How could she tell him she didn't need him to decorate? It was a balm to her prickly conscience that she could think of no way to tell the threesome they weren't needed without hurting their feelings. It even absolved her from some feeling of selfishness on her part.

"My experience in decorating is limited to a few paper ghosts and goblins on the store windows and a pumpkin or two wherever I can find a place to put them. So tell us what you want us to do." He grinned at the boys. "Right, guys?"

"Right." The eager helpers nodded in unison.

Hallie peered at the window reflectively and selected half a dozen leaves and acorns. "Pumpkins and goblins later. Start with these autumn things now. Sort of scatter them on the panes until you think they look right."

She stood back and watched her assistants place a bronzed leaf experimentally in the left hand corner of the pane. When they reset it twice, she moved away to select half a dozen leaves and acorns from the basket.

She placed three leaves before she allowed herself to turn and let her gaze rest on Josh. He was dressed in jeans, a striped cotton shirt and polished loafers. Josh shifted his stance and Hallie quickly turned toward the window before he became aware of her gaze. She repositioned a leaf. She knew it wasn't only admiration that filled her heart. She'd admired him, then liked him and now, the feeling was much stronger. One second her heart was airborne, soaring like a rare eagle; the next, it was dipping toward the earth with the nagging reminder of her career and her impending return to Los Angeles. One didn't easily shelve, even for a day, a dream that had grown since she was a teenager.

Her gaze roved back to Josh, wondering if Marianne found Josh as attractive as she did—if Marianne allowed herself to see him as more than a kindergarten room father. It wasn't unlikely. Maybe Marianne took Robby to the lake to play with Josh with more on her mind than the boys' friendship.

She turned to watch the trio. Just watching Josh and

Nate made her heart swell like a balloon. Not to mention the thought of going home with them to fix spaghetti and help with the dishes and have coffee on the balcony, which was absurd. She was a substitute teacher. That was all. Just because Josh had given her the glass globe with the family snow scene didn't mean he wanted her for a substitute mother, let alone a wife. He might trust her with his son, briefly, but not with his heart.

Josh secured a leaf to the pane and stepped back to peer at the boys' handiwork. "What do you think?" He stepped back from the array of autumn decorations sparkling as the afternoon sun caught the slight sprinkle of glitter Hallie had added earlier.

Hallie tilted her head, aware Nate and Robby awaited her approval. She squinted her eyes, nodding slowly, careful not to let the smile bubbling behind her lips burst forth too quickly. Decorating was serious business. "Very nice. If the school had a contest for the best decorated room, we'd win hands down." She freed the waiting smile, looking at the radiant faces of the youngsters, careful not to glance at Josh. A shared look would undo her. She picked up another cluster of leaves, letting her heartbeat settle into place.

She held the leaves up. "Is Marianne picking up Robby here?" she asked conversationally.

"At the store, in case we'd left before she arrived. You know how doctor's appointments are." Josh glanced at his watch. "Oops. She may get there before us at the rate we're going."

"We can stop whenever you like," Hallie said, wishing they could decorate forever.

"Paul will be getting the late afternoon crowd."

Hallie nodded, returning the leaves to the basket. "Thanks for staying to help." Her eyes focused on the boys, but her mind was on Josh. "We got a lot done."

The kindergartners accepted her thanks with a quick nod, uttered a hasty 'bye, and started for the door to the classroom without a backward glance.

"Television or games," Josh said apologetically.

Hallie nodded in understanding. "Thanks again."

"I hate to leave." Josh's gaze affirmed his words. "But Paul and a crowd of customers may be waiting for me. And I left spaghetti sauce in the crockpot." He lifted a hand. "See you, soon."

Not soon enough, Hallie thought. She smiled and waved and knew she could leave and get some writing done before dinnertime. But the appeal of the computer screen was lost as she envisioned a room overlooking the lake and the aroma of spaghetti sauce wafting across the table of a family of happy diners. She lifted the leaves again. She might as well decorate the windows of her classroom.

Hallie pulled her car into the lighted parking lot of the country store, knowing that the absence of cars didn't mean Josh had no customers. Many of them walked from the campground to the store. But it was near closing time, so he might not be busy. She secured the parking brake.

She couldn't deny the class trip was an excuse to

see Josh. Talking to him at school had been difficult; she was monitoring children or chatting with another parent when he left Nate or picked him up. Which he seemed to use as an excuse for rapid departure, as if he was avoiding an allergic reaction to her.

She could have discussed the proposed class trip to a market. A local, open-air market had constructed an imaginative display of pumpkins, stair-stepped along two walls to form a pyramid in one corner. She wanted Josh's opinion about Nate attending the outing. And his company on the trip, she admitted. Hopefully, few customers would be lingering in the aisles. A soft evening breeze ruffled her hair as she stepped from the car and walked across the asphalt.

She opened the door and saw him immediately, standing behind the counter. "Hi, Hallie," Josh greeted her with unexpected ardor. "Are you out of milk again?"

Hallie grinned self-consciously. Then she laughed. "Actually, I do have a reason for driving this way."

"I'd like to think it was to see me."

Warmth flooded her face. Why had she thought he was avoiding her? "Maybe I came to see Nate," she teased.

Josh dipped his head, and Hallie would have thought he looked crestfallen, except he couldn't hide the merriment in his eyes.

"Nate's playing some game with Paul, but if you really want to interrupt them . . ."

Hallie raised one hand quickly. "No, I really did come to see you."

"Ah." Josh looked contemplative. "School. Something to do with the school." He sighed. "And I hoped it was my charm."

Hallie peered at Josh. When had he relaxed? Is this what he was like before he became so wary and responsible and sober? She rolled her eyes toward the ceiling and shook her head with a laugh. "Why are you in such a good mood?"

"Must be the sight of you."

Hallie lifted her gaze heavenward again.

"You need me to decorate again."

Hallie shook her head.

"A field trip?"

"Maybe."

"Do you think we could discuss this on a walk to the lake?"

"The lake?"

"I can close anytime. Paul's with Nate, and I could use a breather."

"I'd like that."

"Just let me tell Paul I'm going to take a walk."

Hallie peered around at the tidy shelves of cans and packages and then Josh was back at her side.

"They scarcely looked up."

Josh closed and locked the double doors and guided Hallie to a side door to exit. They strolled from the lighted parking lot, staying on the narrow road leading past Paul's parents' home, past campers, motor homes and trailers with lights spreading across the darkness. They continued through the pines toward a string of lights and paused at the edge of the lake.

The breeze returned to brush Hallie's cheek and play tag with pine needles, releasing the subtle scent of their fragrance into the air. Water lapped softly against small boats tethered to the shore.

Josh picked up a stone and skipped it across the silver-gray water before he turned to her. "My time is your time. What can I do for you?" he said easily.

Hallie smiled to herself. More than you'd want to, she thought. "I was shopping for groceries—"

"Aha." Josh halted her in midsentence. "My rival for your shopping affection!"

She giggled. "Are you the same man that taunted me about driving to your store for a carton of milk?"

"So where is this store that is more attractive than mine?"

"It's not more attractive than yours. Well," she hesitated, "it does have a pumpkin patch."

"A pumpkin patch makes your heart beat faster."

"No." Hallie looked at Josh in mild exasperation. "I plan to take the class on a trip to a market, and when I saw this pumpkin display, it looked like an ideal place to go in October."

"And?"

Hallie looked up, noticing how the platinum glow from the autumnal moon brushed Josh's cheeks. "There is a spattering of hay amid the pumpkins. I thought I'd better check with you." She shifted her gaze to meet his and the look in Josh's eyes almost made her forget her train of thought. "About Nate going."

"Good idea." Josh's gaze didn't waver.

"Talking to you, or taking the class on the trip?"

"Both." He raised a hand to trail a finger from her cheekbone to her chin.

"Hay doesn't bother Nate?"

"We'll have to talk about that."

"I thought that's what we were doing."

"Among other things."

"What other things?"

"How glad I am to see you."

Hallie breathed in the evening air and felt as if her chest was filled with bubbles. Her throat felt tight and she wondered if Josh, too, felt the same kind of wonderful, tantalizing excitement that teased her senses.

"I thought you'd never admit it."

"What?"

"That you like to see me."

"I always like to see you."

"But you never say it."

Josh didn't reply and the wonderful, tantalizing feeling paled. Had she pushed too far? Had the memory of his wife stepped between them?

"All women aren't the same, Josh."

Josh was silent.

"It's hard to imagine a woman leaving a loving husband and a son who is ill. Because your wife did doesn't mean every woman would."

Josh breathed deeply and turned slightly to look beyond the lake. "Unless she's pushed too far."

Hallie looked at him perplexed.

"It was my fault." Josh hesitated. "Sibyl wanted a child, and when we couldn't have children, I talked

her into adopting a child. I thought a child was supposed to bind a couple together and make their love
stronger." Sadness edged Josh's voice. "I was wrong."
He lifted his head and looked toward the darkened sky
beyond the rustling pine needles. "Adopting Nate
wasn't the same as having her own child, especially
when Nate kept her tied to the house—almost to
him—most of the time. I don't know if she could have
handled a sick child of her own. But with Nate, she
couldn't cope."

"I'm sorry."

"I'm sorry too. For Sibyl, for Nate. I expected too
much of her. I won't do it again."

A stone replaced the earlier bubbles in Hallie's
chest. "Never?"

The sigh of the wind sifting softly through the pine
needles enhanced the sober look on Josh's face.
"Don't think I don't want a mother for Nate. I think
about it every day. A widow with children of her own
who might take on another family."

"A widow?"

Confusion clogged Hallie's mind. *What could a
widow give you that I couldn't?*

"It's not what a widow could give me, Hallie." The
string of lights on the dock bared the pain in Josh's
face. "A widow who has children of her own might
not need to bear more, and could accept my child as
one of a family. Or, at least, that's the way I think."

Hallie narrowed her eyes. *The way you think! How
about the way I think?*

"Hallie, I never meant to lead you on."

Lead me on! Hallie stared at Josh. *If . . . if I fell in love with you, it's my doing.* But she didn't say it. She drew a breath, releasing it slowly while she cleared the angst glazing her eyesight. "You might say I'm the one who threw myself at you." She tried to say it lightly, but she failed miserably. Unable to bear the humiliation, she whirled, taking a step to leave, and was stopped abruptly, held captive by the pressure of Josh's hand on her wrist. "Let me go." The pain in her voice reverberated through her.

"Hallie, I owe you an explanation."

Hallie jerked her arm free. "I've made a fool of myself. Please don't make it worse." She raised her left hand, palm out and closed her eyes for a fraction of a minute. "Don't say anything. Let me go with some dignity."

"Hallie," Josh's voice was ragged. "I love you. More than I can ever tell you." The moan from his throat seemed to echo across the moon-silvered water. For the space of a breath, Hallie waited for his voice to continue.

"I love you enough not to let this go any farther."

Hallie raised weighted eyes. "You think I can't handle Nate's illness? You think I'll leave just because your wife did? That's not giving me much credit, is it?" A sense of frustration welled inside her, threatening to topple her already eroded composure.

"It isn't just Nate's illness." Josh released Hallie's arm and stepped back.

He was silent so long, Hallie peered at him anxiously. "Then what problem is so terrible I would stop . . ." How could she admit her love when he'd practically rejected it? "Stop caring about you?"

"You might not stop caring, but you wouldn't be happy. Just as Sibyl wasn't happy. You might not leave, but I'd see disappointment in your eyes. I don't want to see that in another woman's eyes—especially yours. I'd die inside." He reached one hand forward, but he dropped it before he touched her. "I've seen you with children. With Nate. With the children in your class. You want children of your own someday, right?"

"Don't most women?" Hallie wrinkled her forehead, perplexed.

"Yes, most women do," Josh said softly. "That's the problem."

"It can't be that you don't want any more children. You were extolling the idea of marrying a widow with any number of children."

"Hallie, I'm the one who is sterile. I'm the one who can't give a woman a child."

Hallie blinked, refusing to let her shock show in widened eyes or a slack lip. With careful control, she opened her mouth to speak, but her vocal cords seemed to be injected with some kind of numbing anesthetic. She knew Josh was waiting for her response. She knew she had to say the right words . . . make a positive and supportive reply. Stress sparked an irrational bubble of laughter buried beneath the breath in her lungs, and she knew that was not the right response.

Children—of course, she wanted children of her

own. A child with Josh's beautiful, blue eyes and wonderful caring character traits.

Because he couldn't have children with his wife didn't mean it would be the same with all women, did it? New advances in medicine were announced every day.

In the background she could hear the water and wind and distant laughter from a motor home, but the silence between them loomed as deadly as the air space in a closed tomb. She bent and picked up a pine cone and pressed it into her fingers, remembering the first time a prickly cone had drawn blood and Josh's careful ministrations of first aid. She lifted the cone to her face and inhaled, as if wishing for a strong scent of pine to clear the spinning in her head. But only a faint fragrance, possibly resin, touched her nostrils. She took a steadying breath and raised her lashes. "I can think of worse things."

"Such as?" Josh's voice sounded as if it was raked over jagged gravel.

"Your assumption that we can't be seriously involved because of your problem."

Josh was silent and she looked at him. For a second, so fleeting she knew she must have been wrong, she thought she saw his eyes soften and flare with a ray of hope. Then the glow passed as fleeting as the sigh of wind that stirred a cluster of pine needles overhead. His gaze moved, avoiding her probing eyes.

She wanted him to pull her close and cover her lips with his and tell her everything was all right. She wanted to feel the warmth of his body next to hers, the touch of his hands moving on her back. "Josh, I thought you were beginning to feel the way I do."

He turned at the sound of his name. "Hallie, I love you. I want you." He pulled her into his arms and pressed her against his chest, his breath warm against her ear. "But taking on an ailing child and his handicapped father is more than I would ask." He released her, putting his hands at his side.

She didn't want him to release her, as if somehow the contact would break his resistance. He wasn't giving her a chance. She placed her hands on his shoulders and tilted her head back. "I love you." There, she'd said it. Let him push her away. Gazing at his solemn face, she stood on the tips of her toes and pressed her lips against his, ignoring the little voice that warned her of the crumbling walls of reason. She didn't want to think about future pitfalls.

Like an earlier time, the meeting of their lips sparked a fire like a match touched to a dry bundle of twigs. Instead of Josh pulling away, his lips moved to capture hers with a primitive aggression, teasing the flesh from one corner to the other. His lips pressed against the sensitive surface of her lips, leaving her nerve ends trembling as he molded his body against hers with an intensity that would have startled her, had she not felt the same urge to meld against him.

When he broke the contact with her lips, Hallie clung to him, wondering if she would ever regain a sense of propriety. Wind rustled the pine needles and further away, somewhere amid the mini-homes and trailers and luxurious motor homes, the sound of country-western music drifted toward them.

Hallie breathed carefully, considering her words.

"I'm not against adopting children. Because everyone in a family doesn't look alike doesn't mean they aren't family."

Josh chuckled, albeit shakily. "Don't you think people should talk engagement or marriage before they start on the 'family' thing?"

His effort at levity surprised Hallie momentarily. What surprised her even more was her impulsive response. "Depends on the people." She still felt, somehow, they were teasing, both afraid to leap off a cliff, and yet, she raised on her toes and planted a firm kiss on his lips. "I just wanted you to know how I felt about children."

"I know." There was no laughter in his voice. The moon slid behind a cloud, dimming his face, and Hallie knew instinctively the glow in his eyes had dimmed as well.

"Hallie, I love you and I want to spend my life with you. I want to go to bed with you at night and wake up with you in the morning. I want to celebrate our golden anniversary together. But marrying me is not fair to you."

Fair to me! Hallie was aware her lashes were blinking like caution signs as she pulled away from Josh. With effort, she controlled her lashes, grateful for the cloud-draped moon. This was the Josh she knew— cautious, wary, wounded. But worrying about others— caring, responsible, honorable. She took a determined breath, looked at Josh steadily, and knew her voice would be just as steadfast. "We're right for each other, Josh. I love Nate. I love you. You love me. What more does it take to convince you? I'm not Sibyl. I won't leave." The moon floated past the cloud and glowed in the sky as if to brighten her words.

"You have your writing . . ."

Writing . . . Thoughts of her career were like a wisp of cloud that touched the moon and floated away. "I know a few married writers. Happily married writers."

"Who live together in the same city?"

Hallie was sure the sickening thud she heard was her heart plunging to her heels. "Probably." She didn't want to think about returning to Studio City right now. She wanted to tell him lots of couples had happy marriages and weren't together all the time. She wanted to believe it. She wanted Josh to kiss her again and tell her they could work things out because they loved each other.

But when he did pull her to him again, all the anticipated sensations and tenderness and magic of the kiss didn't forestall the flicker of foreboding that welled up as he pulled away.

"We should get back," he said. "Paul will want to go home." He slid his arm around her shoulder, pulling her against him, and they walked back to the market.

Chapter Ten

Hallie greeted Josh with a warm hello when he came to pick up Nate, controlling an urge to kiss him before half a dozen dawdling students.

"Come for dinner," Josh said.

"Love to," Hallie replied without missing a beat as she handed out a school announcement to the departing class.

"About six. Earlier if you can make it." His look pleaded for earlier as he waved.

Hallie waved at the last student and walked to her desk, stopping beside a large pumpkin. She slid her hand over the satiny surface of the pumpkin, smiling at the memory of the evenings spent with Josh and Nate, carving the pumpkins decorating her classroom. With the aid of stencils and carving knives, the task had ended all too soon for Hallie. Yet, it was the middle of the week—Halloween was just around the corner, and she hadn't planned the field trip. She turned her gaze toward the door and smiled as the school secretary came in.

"Hallie, I like your carved pumpkins, especially the castle. How about doing one for my office?"

Hallie gazed at the carved creation of turrets and battlements of a fantasy castle. They were special. She grinned. "I'll have to confer with my assistants." She looked up. "Did you come down here just to look at my pumpkins?"

"Not exactly." The secretary moved to admire the castellated creation. "You've got a phone call."

For a second, Hallie's mind raced to Nate before she rationalized she'd just seen Nate and he was breathing well. It wasn't like her friends to call her at the school, and her agent never had. But there was always a first time, she thought.

Returning with the secretary to the office, she lifted the telephone with a flicker of anticipation.

"Thought it important enough to call you at the school," her agent said.

Hallie was silent for a lengthy moment while she breathed in and out and lifted her free hand to steady the telephone. Thoughts of Josh receded as she heard the words "script sold." Blood pounded in her ears. Her voice went on a coffee break. She focused on listening to the voice in her ear. "Needs a few changes. When can you be in town to start work on rewrites?"

Hallie replaced the receiver and floated out of the office, vaguely aware that she'd promised to speak to her employer about a replacement. She returned to her classroom on autopilot, knowing she should calm down before she saw her principal. She'd miss her adorable students. She'd miss the mountains. But she'd be back as often as possible. She's already mentioned commuting to Josh. She refused to let *that* dark cloud darken her euphoria. She'd sold a script!

By the time she talked to Lydia, she could speak calmly enough to relay her news and ask Lydia to find a replacement. She was on her way to see Josh minutes later. Waiting impatiently until his customer left, she moved close, slid her arms around his neck and gave him the kiss she'd longed to give him earlier. Before the contact could ignite, she pulled back so she could see his face.

"My script sold." She'd anticipated his smile, but the brilliant beam spreading across his face weakened her.

"I knew it would." He pulled her close again, congratulating her between kisses.

The sound of the market doorbell penetrated her thought a second after Josh suspended his kiss. Hoping her knees would hold her upright, she pulled back, refraining a glance toward the doorway self-consciously. She stepped back from Josh as the customer entered. She felt like a magic mist floated around her. She'd longed for this moment for years.

With the customer perusing the aisles, Josh turned to her. "So, what happens now?"

"My agent says the script needs some work and Lydia is trying to find a replacement for me." She halted as the customer placed two cans of chili on the counter. Barely containing her excitement until the customer was on the way to the door, she continued. "Oh, Josh. It's a dream come true." The glow welling inside her misted her eyes, dulling the knowledge that Josh's smile was fading. "You are happy for me, aren't you? I can commute until you feel Nate can live in the city." Her mind raced with possibilities. "You said your former partner would welcome you back." Even amid her euphoria, fingertips of anxiety tapped at her. She gazed at Josh, willing him not to let the shine in his eyes fade.

"Hallie, you know I'm happy for you." He didn't look at her.

The fingertips drummed steadily now. "I know you bought the store so you could be near Nate all the time." Her voice took on a higher note. "But if we were together, I'd be home with him, writing, while you were at work. Her mind scrambled for options. She couldn't lose Josh. "I can go to school with Nate and write on my laptop in the car." The optimism she'd tried to maintain dwindled at the look on Josh's face.

"Hallie, I know you care for Nate."

"Love Nate," Hallie interjected aggressively.

"I know." Josh sighed. "But it's not just watching Nate. It's the air pollution in the city." He paused. "I tried to tell you."

His words sank in her ears as her heart sunk in her chest. She touched his cheek gently. "I know. I just didn't think you meant *always*." She clung to a wisp of optimism. "I've been working in the mountains during the week and going to the city on weekends.

Maybe I can still do that, if not, I can do it the other way around." She lowered her hand and Josh captured it in his.

"Hallie, I want us to be together. Not just for weekends. I want forever, and forever is not in our future. Nate can't live in the city, and I can't expect you to give up your career. Heaven knows, I want you to. I don't want to lose you. But you've worked so long for your big break . . ."

He paused and took a deep breath. "I know you said you had to live where the work is. I understand that." His look saddened. "But understand me too. I'd go back to the city in a minute if I had only me to think of. But I have Nate. We're a package deal. I couldn't expect any woman to accept all my problems, least of all a woman I love as much as I love you. You have my heart, but I can't give you the rest of me if it must be transplanted to the city. It's not that my love for my son is stronger. I love you more with every breath I take. But Nate needs me. Nate is a responsibility I accepted long ago. I've come to terms with it."

"We can work something out," Hallie repeated stubbornly, enough elation remaining to believe her words.

Josh nodded, smiling weakly. But Hallie knew from the look on his face that he didn't believe her.

Josh watched the taillights of Hallie's car until they disappeared when the car turned onto the highway. She'd stayed until he'd closed the store and put Nate to bed. They'd talked, keeping the conversation light, skirting the main issues. He'd walked her to her car, and all the time, the ache in his chest threatened to still his heartbeat. He didn't want to think that the dreams he had of Hallie in his kitchen, in his bed, in his life, were over.

He trudged up the outside stairs to the balcony.

Involuntarily, his gaze returned to the highway. But no cars passed. The wind sighed through the pine needles and he turned his gaze to the lake. Moonlight sent a swath of silver across the water, like a brush of finger paint from a kindergarten project.

Hallie's dream was coming true while his eroded. He wanted to tell her how much he loved her and needed her. He wanted to hold her in his arms and tell her about his dreams of a future together until she wanted to stay with him as much as he wanted her to stay. He wanted to plead with her to stay with him, to be his wife.

The silver swath on the lake blurred before his eyes, and he wondered how he could bear the pain of Hallie's leaving. But how could he ask her to stay?

He walked inside to Nate's room to watch the rise and fall of his son's ribs beneath the cotton top of his pajamas as he did every night. Nate's breathing was as regular as the ticking of a clock. But the comfort of the regularity didn't ease his pain. Nor did the sight of his son, which usually enriched him with a glow as warm as crackling embers, touch the cold, cube of ice where his heart should be. He turned and walked to the solitary bed awaiting him.

* * *

Hallie had arrived in Studio City Saturday, and the meeting with her friends had led to an impromptu party at the home of one of the writers who lived in an apartment slightly larger than her friend's one-bedroom place. One writer had brought a bottle of champagne from the nearby supermarket to toast her.

"Hallie, will you still remember my name when standing on that stage accepting an award?" Candace teased.

Others threw in chiding remarks about her success, and Hallie glowed and munched on barbecue-sauced meatballs, sipped at champagne in a plastic glass, and reveled in the remarks. But in the back of her mind, she couldn't help wishing Josh was here to celebrate with her.

"I suppose you'll be abandoning my living room couch now." Candace added laughter to her comment.

"Who wouldn't?" someone else chortled. "Hallie can afford to find an apartment in the high-rent district."

Hallie joined the laughter, but something about Candace's choice of words infected the laughter. Josh had congratulated her and told her to have a good weekend, but she couldn't help thinking she'd somehow *abandoned* him. He knew she went to the city on weekends, she told herself. He didn't expect her to stay in the mountains this weekend. He knew she wanted to share her good news with her friends, and she had to start work on the rewrites on Monday.

She let a platter of hot wings pass and accepted a potato chip from a bowl being thrust at her. She chatted with the hostess for a minute. But when the lady moved on, Hallie's thoughts slipped back to Josh.

She could see him every weekend, she consoled herself. Well, every Sunday, anyway. A depressing thought found its way to the surface. Would Josh tire of a long-distance romance? Would he still be looking, unconsciously, for the widow or divorcee with children who would be a mother to Nate and a lover to him? A lover! A pain as sharp as the thrust of a knife touched her chest.

She left the party with Candace, congratulations still sounding in her ears. But the echo of warm voices faded and the glow waned in the early hours of the morning when she turned restlessly on the sofa-bed, her thoughts on Josh. She wanted to be with him, to be able to see him every day. But how could she give up her dream? Or how could she lose Josh? She fell asleep, telling herself it would work out. But she awoke the next morning with a nagging feeling she hadn't settled anything.

On Sunday, she drove back to the mountains, by-passing the turnoff to the market. She wanted to see Lydia before she left for church. She hoped her landlady would let her keep the room for the days she could stay in the mountains. After making arrangements with Lydia, she packed her computer and one suitcase. Leaving part of her clothes made it seem like she wasn't leaving permanently.

She arrived at the market in time to fix lunch for Josh and Nate. But Josh had to eat at his minuscule table in the store. Paul, his usual helper, was with Marianne and her children. Nate, wheezing, was not his energetic self. Business was slow but steady, and every time Hallie tried to tell Josh about the party, his duty at the cash register took priority. Bagging groceries for him seemed to be the only way to stay near him.

They could talk when he closed the store, Hallie thought. But when he locked the front doors and went upstairs with she and Nate, he spent the evening fussing over Nate. At ten, he still didn't have Nate quiet and was worrying if he should take him to the emergency room. By eleven, Nate was asleep and Josh walked to the car with Hallie, kissing her quickly and unsatisfactorily because he couldn't leave Nate alone.

Hallie drove back to Studio City wearily. Josh hadn't said it, but she knew he was thinking, 'I told you what it would be like.' She could see the worry and weariness in his eyes, and the sadness. She wished she could make it go away. Wished Nate could have a normal childhood and she and Josh could have a normal relationship. But wishes were what she'd lived on when she was young. She was an adult now. Wishes didn't come true without help, a lot of help.

Despite arriving in Studio City late, she was up early to see her agent. Candace had already left for her day job.

She spent the morning rewriting and called Josh at noon to ask about Nate's health.

Paul answered. "Josh took Nate to see the doctor." He asked about her work, and she asked about Marianne and the children.

She called again in the afternoon and Paul said they were at the school. Nate couldn't be ill if he was in school, she reasoned. Yet, she wished she was near enough to go and see him. To see Josh. To be nearby if he needed her. She left her number.

Josh didn't return the call until the next evening, after he'd closed the store. He'd been to the school, at Nate's insistence, to deliver a new pumpkin they had carved, to add to the room decorations. Nate was home with a threatening cold. He hung up after a few minutes.

Hallie spent the rest of the week writing, lunching with other writers, and talking writing with Candace when they were at the apartment. She even looked half-heartedly for a two-bedroom apartment.

"Two bedrooms," Candace teased.

"Just in case Josh and Nate should visit." But she knew she was kidding herself. After last Sunday's unsatisfactory visit and the brief telephone call, she wondered if Josh's ardor was being severely tested with second thoughts. Was giving only bits and pieces of her time only prolonging the inevitable time when they would part? His life would evolve around Nate and the mountain community; hers around writing and life in the city. It might work for some, but she wanted more. And she knew Josh wanted more. Would he settle for second best?

Her heart ached with indecision. How could she think about leaving the city now? She'd caught the brass ring. The producer and director liked her story. Her agent *loved* the limo-driver-and-attorney script she was working on. Candace kept saying, "I knew you'd sell first—I'm so happy for you." Acquaintances joined her writing-group friends in calling her on the telephone; others e-mailed her. Some asked for her advice. The recognition was great. She'd been accepted. She wasn't the girl in the thrift-shop shoes hiding behind a palm. Wasn't this what she wanted?

The following weekend, her ancient car had to be towed to a garage for minor surgery, and the telephone calls to Josh were short and unfulfilling.

She was in tears when Candace came in. "How can I be so miserable when I should be walking on clouds?" she wailed.

Candace pulled a tissue from a box and handed it to her. "Maybe the asthma will go away as Nate gets older. I've heard of such things. Then Josh can move back to the city."

"What if Nate's asthma doesn't improve?" Hallie said dismally.

"Hallie, you can't think of giving up writing! Sometimes, even when you're writing is good, you may not get a second chance."

Hallie pressed a tissue against her damp lashes. But would she get a second chance at love?

Candace handed her another tissue. "Put on some fresh makeup and that new dress you bought on Rodeo Drive. We're going out to dinner and see and be seen. You're a screenwriter now."

* * *

By the next weekend, Hallie couldn't wait to get on the freeway out of the city. But Candace insisted she go to a breakfast meeting with several fellow writers.

It was midmorning before she pulled on the freeway. She pressed the gas pedal until she noticed she was passing most of the other cars. She slowed down, reluctantly. She left the tall buildings and densely populated areas and sighed when a patch of greenery on the unsettled hills appeared.

Her thoughts raced ahead to Josh—at the first time she'd seen him standing in the door of her classroom, looking as wary as a warrior—of her momentary anxiety when he'd said he wasn't leaving Nate and her exultation when he'd finally trusted her enough to leave Nate in her care for a few hours. She thought of the night in the hospital with Josh and Nate. Of the trip on the tramway and the way Josh had pulled her near, steadying her in the bumpy moments of the ride. She thought how wonderful it would be to have a steadying hand in her often bumpy life. Or to be a steadying hand. With her thoughts in the mountains, she pressed the brake pedal to slow to a crawl with other cars in the freeway lanes. Twenty minutes later, taillights blinked steadily in all lanes.

Hallie exhaled a huff of air and shifted her gaze beyond the stalled cars. Denuded hills were being leveled for new construction.

Leaning forward, she switched on the radio and found a traffic advisory suggesting drivers turn on the transition road if possible. The announcer reported a tractor trailer, involved in an accident, was blocking freeway traffic in all lanes going east. Traffic might be blocked for hours until the accident scene could be cleared. Hallie switched the radio off and watched an ambulance creep by the stalled cars. A tow truck followed. Highway patrol cars passed. Hallie turned off the car engine.

It was late afternoon when Hallie pulled into the parking lot of the country market. She wanted to rush into the store and throw her arms around Josh's neck and kiss him until he begged for air. She grimaced at the cars parked in the parking lot. So much for wishes! She wilted back against the seat. With luck, she might be able to say hello to Josh before it was time to get in the car and head back to the freeway.

But when she stepped from the car and looked toward the store, her heart soared. Nate fidgeted in the open doorway.

"Miss Ember, I saw you from the window. We've been waiting for you."

Hallie crossed the few yards separating them and bent down, meaning to kiss Nate on the cheek. But he threw his arms around her. "I miss you."

Nate's skin felt soft and warm against her face and he smelled of soap and chocolate. "I wish you'd come back to school."

"I miss you, too, Nate." The door closed behind them as Hallie wrapped her arms around the small body and pressed her lips against his soft cheek. Squeezing her eyes closed to repel the tears threatening to appear, she realized how much she'd missed him and how much she loved him. She cleared her throat enough to speak. "We'd better move away from the door before someone bumps into us." She lifted him in her arms and nudged the door open with her shoulder. She saw Josh as soon as she looked toward the counter. He was looking at her and his eyes were soft and glowing and welcoming. With Nate in her arms, she floated across the floor.

"Look who I found waiting to meet me." She lowered Nate to the floor. "It's great to get a nice welcome."

"We were afraid you weren't coming."

"Neither rain nor snow nor freeway traffic could keep me from getting through," she said cheerfully.

"Traffic heavy?" Josh turned to itemize a variety of groceries for a customer.

"A bad accident stopped all traffic for hours." She squeezed Nate's shoulder, reached for a bag, and placed the items inside after Josh rang them up. She handed the bag to the customer and said good-night.

"Nate, she's getting to be almost as good a helper as you are." Josh gave Hallie a quick wink before he looked down to catch his son's gaze. "Think we could talk her into coming to work for us?"

"We need someone to help, Miss Ember." Nate looked at Hallie eagerly.

"What about Paul?"

Josh laughed. "Alas, Paul is moving into Big Bear near Marianne. "He's going to set up a computer repair service in her garage."

"Ooh," Hallie widened her eyes. "I'm glad to hear it. Even if it does leave you in the lurch, so to speak."

He nodded at a new customer. "Paula is going to help," Josh said.

Hallie reached for a bag and noticed Nate shuffling toward the rec room. She felt a pang of guilt, wondering if he'd thought she was ignoring him, and then a minute later, she heard the sound of voices from the television set. She turned back to bagging groceries contentedly.

Saying good-night to the last customer, Josh took a deep breath and looked at his watch. "It's been a busy day."

"Did you and Nate have lunch?"

He wrinkled his forehead as if trying to recall lunch. "We had packaged sandwiches and ice cream, I think. I mean Nate had the ice cream." He laughed and Hallie heard the weariness in his voice. "How about you?"

"I had a late breakfast."

"Paula put something on to cook in the crockpot for us to eat when I close up. So you will stay for dinner, won't you?"

"Need you ask?"

"I was afraid you'd have to turn around and get back on the freeway," Josh said with evident relief.

Hallie looked at the closing door. "Will you be closing soon?"

"Right now, if that's soon enough. I'd like to see you for more than thirty or so minutes."

Hallie knew her eyes were telling him all her secrets, but she couldn't pull her gaze away. She wanted to see him for more than thirty or so years. At breakfasttime and dinnertime, at bedtime and anytime.

Right now, she wanted him to hold her in his arms and kiss her soundly.

She waited until after dinner, and after Nate had gone to bed, but she got her wish, she thought happily as she returned Josh's kiss. They sat on the couch facing the window open to the darkened view of the lake. They talked about her work and his work and couldn't seem to call it a night.

Josh traced his fingers along her bare arm. "I wish you didn't have to go back to L.A." His look changed, and the light dulled his eyes. His lips tightened for a moment. You could stay and leave early in the morning. I'll sleep on the couch."

Despite his grin, Hallie wondered if he was thinking that a few more hours was only prolonging their parting. Her plan to surprise him by arriving for breakfast lost a little sparkle.

"I don't think it's a good idea to stay in your bedroom. But I was thinking of staying in the mountains and starting for Los Angeles tomorrow."

"You prefer the couch?" he teased.

"I kept my room at Lydia's."

"You're going to wake her up at midnight?"

"I have a key, but I called her while you were getting Nate settled. I called Candace as well."

Josh pulled her close and kissed her lightly. "That's interesting." His lips moved downward, pausing briefly at the hollow of her throat.

Hallie turned her head to catch his lips when they traveled upward again. Embers flared, withering thoughts of the city and her writing—and the indecisions that had plagued her daily. She was engulfed in a paradise that rivaled anything she could put on paper.

"I still wish you didn't have to go back to L.A.," Josh said when he released her mouth.

The small clock on the wall showed midnight when a coughing sound came from Nate's bedroom. When Josh returned to the room, Hallie was standing.

"Time for me to go," she said reluctantly. She raised her lips, longing for a lingering kiss, but their lips touched all too briefly.

"It's times like this that tell me I should have listened to that little warning voice the first time I kissed you," he said, with a note of sadness. "But how could I not fall in love with you?"

He walked her to the car and kissed her cheek. "See you in the morning." He was back inside, hurrying to see if Nate was stirring, before she had the headlights on.

Letting herself into Lydia's house, Hallie walked softly upstairs. She read the note Lydia had left and put it aside. She brushed her teeth, found a gown, and sank dreamily onto the bed. The feeling was brief. Reality was only a breath away.

Josh's parting words echoed in her head. 'I should have listened to that little warning voice . . . but how could I not fall in love with you?'

Was he telling her a lasting relationship couldn't survive with the thought of her leaving hanging over every minute they spent together? Or did he see her as leaving every time Nate had a breathing problem?

Nate had been wheezing both times she'd left. Did the vision of Sibyl still haunt him—taunt him—with the prospect that Hallie would do the same?

Unable to sleep, she slipped from the bed and sat by the window, listening to the sighing of the pine needles stirring in the mountain air.

An agony of indecision clawed at her. The prospect of parting forever with Josh left pain as deep as if talons had ripped at her heart.

But how could she give up her career in the city? It had taken years to sell a screenplay. Realizing her dream had taken even longer. There was no way she could give it up. She closed her eyes and leaned back in the chair. At daylight, she dressed and went down-stairs.

"In response to your note," she told Lydia cheer-fully. "Yes, I can fill in this morning for the teacher that called in. After I have breakfast with Josh."

Lydia's smile showed both gratitude and relief. "I wouldn't ask, but she called so late, I'm not sure I could find someone. I wish you could say that for the whole term," Lydia said. "You're subbing for the teacher you replaced. She has a problem with her baby and plans to stay home."

Hallie made a sympathetic sound as she waved. "I'll be in the classroom on time," she promised cheerfully. "Oh, yes, and I need to make a telephone call some-time this morning, if you could relieve me for a few minutes."

She had coffee and rolls with Josh in the store, wait-ing anxiously for a break in customers so she could talk to him. But a break didn't come, and she had to leave and she hadn't told him she was teaching the morning class. She hadn't told him about her long, sleepless night.

Despite the usual activity of the morning students, Hallie's thoughts rehashed the turmoil of the early morning hours. But she didn't doubt her decision. Just seeing Josh for a few minutes this morning was wonderful. And Lydia had capped the decision with the offer of a full-time job.

Waiting for Josh to appear in the doorway was as nerve-wracking as Hallie's first day in the kindergarten classroom. Then the door opened, and Josh stood in the doorway, the autumn sun gilding his hair.

Their gaze met. The solemn contours of his face shifted. No longer the wary father, his eyes, his cheeks, his lips wavered, and the radiance of his countenance dimmed everything in Hallie's view.

Slowly, he shifted his gaze, allowing her to regain her composure while he watched his son find a name-tagged bin. Then her heart soared as he turned his gaze back to her and crossed the room.

"I thought you left for L.A." His gaze held her captive.

"Nope."

"Not leaving today?"

"Not leaving today, not leaving tomorrow. . . ." Hallie wrinkled her forehead mischievously. She saw the question flicker in Josh's eyes.

"You're planning to live in the mountains."

Hallie nodded slowly, meeting Josh's expectant gaze.

"Miss Ember," Nate danced around her. "Are you going to be our teacher today?"

Hallie grinned, looking aside to see some of her students look up from putting their things in the bins. "Today and the rest of the term." The yelp of joy from her students overwhelmed her.

Josh looked at her with another question in his eyes.

"The teacher I was replacing wants to stay home with her baby."

"What about your career? Your fifteen minutes of fame . . . your moment on the stage accepting an award . . . your acceptance by your colleagues?"

Hallie grinned. "I had a minute of fame when the manuscript was accepted."

"You can give up writing?"

"I called my agent this morning." She swallowed, remembering the dismal conversation. "We agreed I'd finish the rewrites by e-mail and come into the city only if necessary. He wasn't happy." Unable to resist any longer, she touched Josh's arm. "The important thing in my life is being with you and Nate. As for writing, when I get an overwhelming urge, I'll finish the novel I started in college."

Josh looked at her solemnly. "You're sure about this?"

"I'm sure," Hallie said firmly. She was. The acceptance she needed was in Josh's eyes, and the eyes of the child she'd come to love.

Josh gazed at her, his eyes filled with love. "I'll be back to pick up Nate . . . and you, after class."

"I'll be here." Hallie said. Despite the youngsters bouncing and shuffling around her, she raised on her toes and pressed a quick kiss on Josh's lips. "I'll improve on that when I get to the store." She made a tiny grimace. "That is, if you don't have a room full of customers."

"I'll put a 'closed' sign on the door."

Laughing, Hallie touched his cheek. "You'd better go before I forget I'm a kindergarten teacher. I may need this job for a while."

Josh leaned close to her ear. "Not too long, I hope. I don't believe in long engagements," he said softly.

"Is that a proposal?"

"I'll do better, later." He pulled away a few inches, gazing into her eyes. "Have I told you I loved you today?"

"Not in words," Hallie said gaily.

"I love you, Hallie Ember."

Aware of the milling students, Hallie forced her fingers not to reach out and touch Josh. "No more than I love you, Josh Snow." She knew the look in her eyes emphasized her words, and she grinned. How could she have once thought of this warm, loving kindergarten dad was a chilly snowman?

Her heart soared. They had the rest of their lives to melt any remaining snowflakes with the carefully tended embers of their love.